D1043696

# TRIPLE
# THREAT

# RELENTLESS AARON

St. Martin's Paperbacks

Relentless Aaron, Relentless Content, and Relentless are trademarks of Relentless Content, Inc.

TRIPLE THREAT

Copyright © 2004 by Relentless Aaron.

Cover photo © Barry David Marcus.

ISBN: 0-312-94966-9
EAN: 978-0-312-94966-2

Printed in the United States of America

Relentless Content, Inc. edition published 2004
St. Martin's Paperbacks edition / February 2008

St. Martin's Paperbacks are published by St. Martin's Press, 175 Fifth Avenue, New York, NY 10010.

10 9 8 7 6 5 4 3 2 1

## SPECIAL DEDICATIONS

This book is inspired by all of the crazy, sexy, cool women in my life. No question: you all know who you are! To the many radio personalities throughout the country who have supported Relentless: Thank you for giving my words a voice. Bugsy, Champaign, Lenny Green, Chaila, Jeff Foxx, Talent and Bob Slade (Kiss FM/NY) . . . Thank you, Wendy Williams, for recognizing true talent. And a Good Morning to you, Ms. Jones and Ms. Info, New York's Dynamic Duo. Thank you to the homies in Philly: Glen Cooper, Golden Girl, Q-Deezy, Tiffany and S.O.L., Colby Cobe, Patty Jackson; in Louisiana (KVEE), Eric.

**Super thanks to:**
**G-Unit Clothing Co., Vitamin Water, and**
**Louis Royer Sponsors of**
**the Relentless brand**

*As always:* To my friend and mentor: Johnny "George Dub" Williams. Thank you to Tiny Wood (my close friend and confidant): Still waiting to have that "Chess Night." To my friends at Allenwood FCI, Otisville FCI, Fort Dix FCI and other prisons throughout the country: Thank you for your support in my personal struggle to be me, to be free, and to be progressive. I hope I represent all you can be.

### KEEP YOUR HEADS UP AND HOLD ME DOWN!

**To Julie and Family:**
(I know I can . . . be what I wanna be . . . if I
work hard at it . . . I'll be where I wanna be!)

**To Emory and Tekia Jones:**
Can you believe this??? Spit in the wind,
and you might create a thunderstorm! (D.B.D.)
Thank you for your support.

To AB, Chris Lighty, Ajuba, and Ian Klienert. To Earl Cox, thanks for sharing industry secrets with me. Thank you, Sidi and Omar (125th St.). To Carol and Brenda (C&B Books) . . . can you guys keep up with me??? To my inner circle: Curt Southerland, Darryl, Adianna, DTG, Tiny, Garnell, Rick, Sadia Demetrius, Angel, Renee Mc Rae,

Mechel . . . To Ashleigh, we sure came a long way in a short time! You go girl!

To Makeda Smith at Jazzmyne Public Relations, my publicist, banker, diva and therapist . . . thank you ever so much. And stay away from the matched! Special thanks to Stephanie Renee, the mogul from Philly . . . To Shakia: Did you think I forgot? Mr. Perkins, Petee (thanks for the street hustle), Ruth, Lucinda, Andrew, and John.

And how could I ever forget you, Renee? You're on fire and I'm burning up!

Thank you all.

To the many bookstores and Web sites and others around the world who carry Relentless Content: Thank you for affording me space on your shelves. I intend to cause a major increase to your bottom line.

**Special thanks to Shetalia and Alese.**
**Luv you guys.**
"We is one." You're in the house now, girls.
Represent!

And, last but not least,
to my earth, moon and star:
**Paulette, DeWitt and Fortune**
Love you guys to death.

# FOREWORD

APRIL DAVIS is a woman whom you've gotta love. She has big, beautiful brown eyes that immediately tell you it's okay to talk to her. Her smile is as humble as it is hearty—a combination that one could only be born with. A loving, compassionate soul, April always gives 110 percent.

SISSY DICKERSON is April's best friend. She's pretty, with a tight G.I. Jane physique, and she's been with the New York City Police Department for years. Sissy usually gets her way, whatever it takes, mainly because of her inner strength, her determination and undying passion. But Sissy also has some issues. Her Teflon-tough attitude makes it hard to be social. It's a barrier that's been nourished by all the tragedy in her life thus far. It's also made her a headstrong avenger. When she's on the beat, helping others, or fighting crime, she's also satisfying some of her own issues.

Finally, there's RIVER RENÉ BURLINGTON, a very bitter, very deceitful murderess. As much as she loves her men she's also killing them and getting away with it. But now that Sissy is so close to catching River, there are some surprises in store.

# RIVER RENÉ BURLINGTON

CALL ME CRAZY, but I'm getting really good at this, to the point that I can say I enjoy killing. It's men who I get the most pleasure out of executing, stabbing and poisoning, among other things. But I've recently come to realize that killing a woman can be just as pleasurable. I guess that bitch, Officer Sissy Dickerson, would call this latest escapade a double homicide. But to me, it was just a simple case of some girl getting in the way; in the wrong place at the wrong time.

For this particular encounter, I picked up this producer named Barry Fuller at Nola's, a swanky nightclub in midtown, on 52nd Street, close to Broadway. We didn't actually meet at Nola's, it was just a rendezvous that we agreed on the night before when I attended a music industry function at The Supper Club. Don't ask me how I managed to be around all of those hotshot celebrities.

Maybe it was dumb luck, if that's what you wanna call it. But Barry slipped me a note that night while he made small talk.

"Don't look at it now," he told me. "It's a surprise."

So I didn't. I forgot all about, it until I undressed later at home. In front of Barry, I had slipped the folded cocktail napkin into my bra, tryin' to be all sexy about it. Huh. Was that really necessary, considering how easy men are to seduce these days? And why in the world was I trying to seduce him, anyway? Well, for one thing, I was horny, he was semi-attractive and, well . . . he was a producer after all. An accomplished one, too. He even won an award that night at the Supper Club. And isn't it a girl's dream to wind up with a rich, successful man?

Okay, so maybe it's a far-fetched fantasy, seeing as how those so-called rich and successful men are so few in comparison to all of us single, horny women. Add to that, if you're a black woman with issues, the odds against you are greater. Better have good looks to fall back on, or else . . . or else it would be a stroke of luck. A wait to exhale.

But me and Barry? It was just dumb luck. Like we stumbled on each other. I knew he was a pushover the moment I met him—half-stuttering, with a film of perspiration there on his brow. He even fumbled with the wad of money he held, or tried to hold, dropping it on the floor where we stood near the bar in the crowded club. He had a bit of a belly, he wore wire-framed glasses and his hair was cut close to the scalp. I liked his lips: full, but not so fleshy. Plus there was an instant when I imagined them on me. We had the same brown complexion too, so it didn't take much to attract me to him.

This could turn out to be something big, I told myself. And I'm being honest when I say the run-in at Nola's was, for me, mere foreplay. I had already made my decision the night before—I always do that when I see a man. Would we work out in the bedroom? Would he fit inside of me, or is it too big? Could we take this thing all the way to the altar? How would our children look? And then the "yes" or "no" decision would be made right there. No second thoughts. Sure, this was all hopeful thinking, but shit, I'm twenty-four years old these days. And my so-called biological clock is ticking. I can't be a free agent all my life.

Needless to say, my producer-friend came to Nola's with nostrils flaring. I had on Chanel perfume, a Wonderbra that made my breasts bubble out of my black top, and a body-hugging green skirt that covered just half of my thighs. My fishnet stockings always got a lot of attention anytime I wore them; I know this from other occasions, how my look was playing on men's imaginations. The effect was dazzling, like there were a dozen black spiders climbing up my legs, trying to get to my diamond mine. Either that, or men were thinking I had a bit of whore hidden in me.

Beyond how my body was clothed, I had on my black stilettos and a sunlight-blond wig with the hair falling into slight curls near my lower neck. No question, I was scandalous!

It was getting late and I was getting edgy, so I just cut to the chase. "Okay, Barry, so level with me. I've had two drinks, you've had one. We've talked about what we do for a living—you the music, me the office manager. We've discussed failed relationships, our families, our futures . . . maybe we're all talked out by now. But I want you to be frank with me. Are you interested? Am I someone you'd like to get to know better?" The face I made should've said a million and one things; most of all that I wasn't playing games.

"Wow. So direct, River, aren't you?"

"I like direct. It pushes aside all of the bullshit. And to be honest, Barry"—I took his hand—"I usually like to take the car on a test drive before I decide to buy it."

"Ooooooh . . . spontaneity, huh?"

"I like spontaneity. There's a lot of truth in spontaneity. It comes from the heart."

"A test drive . . ." He chuckled some under his breath before saying, "That sounds exciting."

I said, "And I'm all about excitement."

That's all it took. Barry and I left Nola's in a chauffeur-driven town car. It wasn't a limo, but then I found out that Barry was conservative. A lot of platinum hits under his belt, and plenty of cash and credit to go with it. But still, the man spent money practically, not lavishly or carelessly. I liked that too, because if this thing between us went any further than one night, it could mean our girl River would always be flowing in dough. The more money he saved, the more there was for me to spend. Hee hee.

Before I know it we were driving north along the Saw Mill River Parkway until we reached Hartsdale. Never been to this town before, but I'd seen one or two newspaper ads for car dealerships, a furniture outlet, and the latest audio-video wholesaler that claimed their prices were "INSANE!" From the parkway, the town car snaked through the suburbs for ten minutes until we turned into an oval driveway.

"Wow. I'm impressed already. And you live here alone?"

"Just me and my little kitty cat, Daddy's Girl."

"Daddy's Girl? Is that a name?"

"It is now," he said. And I laughed like a silly college coed, wondering secretly if this man was just pretending to be naïve, or whether he was a touch crazy underneath.

No matter. I had Sally with me, in my purse. Whenever in doubt, always take Sally out. But who was I kidding? Lately I never left home without her. Especially in this day and age, with the cast of wackos on the rise.

Barry unlocked the front door and let me in the

low-lit foyer to his home. He closed the door behind me. I turned to him after taking an eyeful of the grand entry hall. It was dark, but grand nonetheless. I hadn't even turned all the way around before Barry pushed me back against the wall, his body pressed full up against my own, and his lips all but devoured mine.

I was thrust up against the wall and could hear my body's thump along with my own breathless sigh. Unsure of what was happening to me and overcome with fright, I patted around for my purse, looking for Sally. I couldn't believe how Mister Nervous and Conservative turned into such an animal so quickly. *Fuck!* I told myself, assuming that I had been tricked.

And then, between kisses, Barry uttered his unfounded testimonies, as is "I've been . . . waiting . . . all night to be able to be alone . . . with you . . . oh River!"

Thank God, this was just the man's lust and passion taking over. My distress turned to a kind of high anxiety, where I was more than happy to oblige Barry's desires with my own aggressive measures. I didn't put up the wall like we were taught to do from our early years: "Don't let the boys go too far . . . you don't wanna seem too easy . . ." The hell with that. I grabbed his balls in a way that was possessive and at the same time violent. He let out a grunt that was fed into my mouth like warm gas. Soon our hands were groping at each other like fiends, pulling at belts, buttons and other accessories.

The high-speed striptease was followed by Barry carrying me up a flight of stairs and into a room so dark it didn't matter. It could've been a black hole for all I cared. This was pleasure, to be swept off my feet like I was, surprised by this absolute animal.

Yes! Take me!

The man's lips were foreign against my breasts, my nipples, and further down until he buried his head between my legs. I thoroughly enjoyed this man's daring. After all, he didn't know me so well as to get so far, so fast. But then, since he was willing to go there . . . to satisfy me like he was . . . who was I to complain? Soon I was calling out his name like it was candy on my tongue, begging him not to stop. And he obeyed, so it was more than cool.

I worked up a fever so hot and heavy that I was about to come all over this guy's face . . . about to let out my heartiest scream ever. Something the heavens might hear.

"You—fucking—bastard!"

When I heard the words I smiled at the idea. The man was talking dirty already! But no, that was a woman's voice! And I opened my eyes to see that the bedroom light was on. Shit. Just when I was gettin' my rocks off.

"Fuck!" Barry exclaimed.

"Fuck? Is that all you have to say? Fuck?" The woman was this short, thin, redheaded bitch, and I swore I could see steam comin' off her head. Suddenly, this man's tongue on my pussy wasn't all that exciting anymore.

"I'll show you fuck," the redhead said. Then she ran off to God knows where.

"Who's that?" I asked. Barry wagged his head at me and went to pull his pants on.

"Well? What are you, stupid, you fucking whore? That's my wife." Barry threw my clothes at me and said, "Wrap it up. The party's over."

I was still lying there naked, propped up on my elbows, with my legs apart as if some outrageous encounter had transpired. And hadn't it? *Whore? No you didn't call me a whore!* I scrambled into my clothes, more than prepared to kick this fool in the dick before calling a cab.

"Jane!" Barry lumbered out of the room like a klutz before I could get all of my clothes on. A moment later I picked up the phone and dialed 411.

"Can I have a cab company in Hartsdale, please?" When the operator gave me the number I dialed and asked that a car be sent to—"Shit!" I exclaimed, suddenly aware that I didn't know the address. "Hold on, ma'am. Please." I hurried out of the bedroom and down a hallway toward the stairs. Yelling was a constant back-and-forth down there. I couldn't see the two, but I heard enough to know that I didn't belong here.

"She's just a whore, baby. Don't give up on us for a piece of ass."

"Fuck you, you bastard! This is the last time! If you can't keep your dick in your pants, I'm gonna help you. When I'm finished with you there ain't gonna be no dick left! Nothing but a stub! Now let me by before I start cutting you to pieces."

"Where you goin,' Jane?"

"I want the whore!"

I made it to the bottom of the steps when Barry's wife appeared.

"I'll teach you to fuck with a married man, you home-wreckin' whore!"

Jesus! The woman had a kitchen knife that was long enough to be a pirate's sword.

"Miss! Control yourself! I don't want your man!"

But my words fell on deaf ears. Short Shit was comin at me, knife in hand. I was wide-eyed and my chest was heavy with a banging heart. I saw my purse on the floor where Barry had pushed me against the wall . . . where I had dropped it once I had realized that this would be lust and not violence. Wow, was I ever wrong about that!

Next thing I know, I was diving for my purse. The woman hesitated for a moment, not sure what I was up to. If she didn't know then, she'd know now.

"Now slow your roll, bitch. Slow your goddam roll." I was able to direct the snub-nose at Short Shit just in time.

"Jane, please." Now Barry emerged from behind

the woman, eventually getting the full picture. "A gun? You bring a fucking gun into my house?" The way he came at me was as if he didn't think I'd use the weapon.

"Well, you know us whores. We like to be protected from lyin'-ass, pussy-lickin' womanizers like you."

Just then, the redheaded Short Shit lunged at me. Maybe she thought she'd be faster than me . . . and why she was risking her life over some lowlife, I don't know. But that was beside the point. It was my life that was at stake here. As much as I didn't want to, I pulled the trigger. All I saw was the splatter of dark red mix with the orange-red hair on her head. The woman was thrown back to the floor; the bullet had made an open gash in her where her eyebrow use to be.

"She asked for it," I said calmly, as if I needed to explain myself to her lame-ass husband. Barry went to the woman's side at once. A moment later, he turned his angry eyes at me. I saw the knife in his hand and I snapped. I emptied the gun until the center of the man's chest turned to alphabet soup.

I thought quickly about the things I might've touched while here at this man's home, but things had happened so fast that there wasn't time to touch much. I thought about the address, the phone . . . oh God, the phone. I wondered if the operator had heard the commotion as I raced up the steps barefooted. The line was dead. Shit. This was a first. Not one dead body, but two. Okay, River René Burlington. Calm the fuck down. Been here, done this. The operator probably just hung up because I took too long. Relax. Breathe in . . . breathe out. That's right. Okay, good. Now for the address.

I had to poke my head outside to look over the doorway. There was the number . . . 16. I recalled that this was Black Cherry Lane. I went back to the same phone up in the bedroom for two reasons: to call the operator and ask for the taxi again, and to wipe the fingerprints from it. I was tempted to find a fireplace and burn the phone, just to make sure. But instead I rubbed the receiver real good, and even found hair grease to dress it with. In case there was some other last-minute cleaning to be done, I took the jar with me downstairs.

A minute or so later, I found myself standing in the entry hall awaiting my fate. It would either be the police or a taxicab to pick me up. In the meantime, I drew a lipstick heart on the cheeks of my black and white victims, and then I sat at the foot of their winding stairway and reviewed my work. There was a puddle now where the blood of both bodies had merged. I made light of the situation, joking with myself as I wondered if when type A blood mixed with type B blood, it became type C. The thought amused me, and I laughed out loud so that my lone voice filled the cavernous entry hall.

"See, Barry? Now if you woulda kept my black

ass in the city . . . maybe if you took me to one of those expensive hotels somewhere, maybe then our friend Sissy would've taken the case—she's hot on my trail, ya know. But noooo . . . Mister Two-timing Bastard had to show off his pretty suburban home. Now look where it got you. Dead. You and red, dead—ha ha!

> *"You gave me head*
> *And then came red*
> *And now you both are dead!*

"Wow, Barry. That rhymes." I laughed real hard at my sick humor. I swear I crack me up.

Soon there was a motor running outside. A car horn sounded. And I looked outside through a window to find that—whew!—it was a taxi. I checked my wig and sunglasses in the entry-hall mirror, and with my scarf I turned the knob and let myself out of the Fuller home. Such interesting hosts those two were.

The cabdriver made small talk but I made like I was exhausted with a bunch of murmurs and other discouraged responses as he took me to the Bronx.

"Here's good," I told him as we came to the intersection of Fordham Road and Webster Avenue.

"Are you sure? It looks dangerous out here for a pretty lady like you."

When he said that I considered a direct response, like, I bet your bedroom would be safer, wouldn't it? "Keep the change," I said after slipping him the folded money. Then I got out and watched him disappear. Thank God.

I walked for three blocks to Third Avenue, and entered through the back entrance of my building. I remember being relieved to have gotten away with murder. Again.

Before long, I was snug in my crib where I could finally relax. I found myself missing that man's tongue between my folds. He seemed so experienced! I had to have Brandon to come and finish the job. I whistled before I called out to him, "Come, Brandon. Come to River." Brandon is my Labrador retriever. He's got a completely golden coat of hair and sharp black eyes. He also obeys like the man I never knew. "Attaboy. Take care of Momma like only you can."

Barry and Jane Fuller were my seventeenth and eighteenth victims. I'm batting a thousand. I'll take a day's rest and return Victor's call. He'll be the usual: a movie, dinner, and he'll wanna get in my panties. By the end of the night he'll have satisfied my cravings . . . my cravings for sex and blood.

# SISSY DICKERSON

IT TOOK SIX months for me to get my transfer from the 77th precinct in Brooklyn to the 52nd Precinct in the Bronx. The whole idea was to escape the daily torture; from my so-called fellow officers to the lawlessness of the streets, it was just too much for me to handle. Sometimes I've gotta remind myself that I am a woman. And, although I'd like to hold up the torch for all of us as the be all to end all of civilization, I know that we too have limitations. All day long I have to have this tough-as-nails mentality, just to be able to protect myself from so much nonsense. If it's not this officer or that wanting to take me out for a drink, then it's the others who keep that womanizing air behind their eyes. Chauvinist pigs, all of 'em.

"Keep yo' head up, Dickerson."

"Maybe one day you'll make lieutenant." Blah, blah, blah.

But I can read right through the mess. I hear the snickers. I know about the good ole boy conversations in the locker room. The ones who think they can earn the pussy keep trying, whether it's by confidence games, good deeds, or straight patience. The ones who know they ain't got a chance in hell are enemies. The only thing keeping them from spitting on me is our uniform. The so-called code of honor. Ha. Honor this middle finger. I see right away, whoever I deal with on the force, that I have to show them my no-nonsense attitude. The mask.

But really, I'm a sensual woman. I'm sexy when I need to be . . . when I wanna be. Thing is, I can't wear that hat all the time. I definitely can't wear it on the job. And frankly, I haven't been feeling men lately.

The streets of Brooklyn are the other half of my issues. Black people are killing themselves out here every day. It's like we don't want each other to live. We don't even want each other to advance, at least not further than ourselves. Day after day there's shootings, stabbings, robberies, and assaults. It got to a point where I can't even help those who really need it. A lost child is no longer the same priority as a homicide. Giving a person directions has become a frivolous task next to a breaking and entering; or, more often than not, it's a black-on-black thing. At least in Brooklyn it was.

So I put in for the transfer. And, as if to put icing on the cake, one night I had to witness a car jump the curb. The driver was drunk and lost control of the vehicle. I heard a scream and some grunts and the crashing of a car into a storefront. I could've been every female superhero—Wonder Woman, Batgirl, whatever—and still I wouldn't have been able to help the worst of those victims laid out on the sidewalk. The woman who I was eventually staring down at had her limbs twisted back and around like awkward branches, one eye was turned up so that only the white showed, and there was a deep, bloody wound where her ear had been.

I was frozen. I couldn't get myself to bring the radio-mic to my lips. A bystander had to come and help me, much less the real victims. I had seen gunshot wounds, assault victims; I've helped to deliver a baby—in an elevator and a fast food restaurant. To say the least, I've witnessed my fair share of blood. Of violence. But never like this. Never like this poor woman's brains spilling out of her head. She could've been plain ole roadkill; only on the sidewalk.

My transfer couldn't have come soon enough. I was around a few more like me at the 52nd. Black women. Latinas, a few white girls. Of course there were men, but here they seemed to be more accepting of the idea of a woman by their side to help fight the war on crime and confusion. I think back to my days at the 77th from time to time, wondering if I could've made it past a year without getting shot. Or worse.

Fact is, it's a jungle out there. Brooklyn, I swear, was a real gangland at times. It has its nice areas, but when the sun went down, surviving was not for the weak or kindhearted. In other words, the car that jumped the curb and the lady with her head busted open were events I should've been able to shrug at. I should've been able to go and have a drink with the guys . . . just forget the whole bit. Tomorrow's another day. I couldn't now that I had this new environment, and Maritza Garcia as my new partner, I felt as though I could take on the job with a little more comfort. I thought I had left the horrors behind.

Maritza's my girl, fo' real. She's something of a fun-loving Puerto Rican mami who balances a degree of sexiness with a hard-core round-the-way-girl attitude. You wouldn't wanna get on her bad side. There's this sense about her that if you ticked her off, and if she couldn't fix the problem herself, a whole army of brothers, sisters and cousins would come to her aid in the wink of her Spanish eye. My thinking that could've had something to do with her always bringing her family up in the conversations we'd have during our daily grind. It just so happened that Maritza's old partner was also transferred, leaving an opening for a sidekick. Me.

"SO, WHY YOU get transferred?" Maritza's heavy Latin–New Yawk accent almost had me bustin' out laughing. So spicy . . . so ghetto.

"Actually, I'm from the Bronx. Parkchester," I responded.

"Okay, girl." Maritza sucked her teeth. "I live over on Westchester and Tremont."

"Near Motor Vehicles?"

"You got it. Maybe we can do the car pool bit."

"Yeah, when I get a car—"

"Oh, my bad. I thought that was yours."

"I wish. I turn it in tomorrow. I was just renting it to move my things back up here."

"Where you live now?"

"Next to St. Barnabas."

"The best hospital in the Bronx. I had my baby girl there." Maritza took one hand off of the steering wheel and pulled out a photo from the breast pocket behind her badge. The baby looked something like a piglet. A peach, with beady eyes.

"Oh! She's so cuuuute!" I lied.

"Eight pounds. But that was two months ago. We gonna get some of those professional photographer jobs next week. My cousin does that kind of work."

"That's good to know," I lied again.

"You got kids?"

"No. I haven't been lucky enough to find a partner. I don't want a lover, a husband or a boyfriend either. Just a donor. Just drop off your seed and keep it movin'."

Maritza laughed and said, "Oh my God, you are so funny. Drop off your seed—" And she broke into laughter again. But I was as serious as a four-alarm fire. A man was the last thing I needed.

OUR RELATIONSHIP GREW into a semi-friendship. I say semi because way in the back of a police officer's mind there's a neon sign flashing against those dark walls. It says "Don't Become Close . . . Don't Become Close." And the message switches on effortlessly whenever we do, almost, become close. There's this idea that overshadows many of us, how if we become friends we'll let the relationship interfere with our job . . . and that that same state of mind might possibly get that officer killed. Then you lose a partner and a friend. So the best prevention is to nip it in the bud. Don't let the seed grow into more than just another weed. You can't miss what you never had.

Maritza was already handling domestic disturbance calls, and besides that, she had her own squad car. So, me being still wet behind the ears, I was fortunate to avoid the whole flatfoot routine— marching up and down Fordham Road, White Plains Road or (God forbid) Jerome Avenue during the dead of night—and I fit in conveniently to assist her with those calls.

I never fought in any war, and I didn't yet experience the notorious "battle zone": bullets flying, commands shouting and mayhem. However, if there was danger to be experienced, then it was my

daily grind to swim in it. There comes a point
when the crying babies, the couples shouting and
the dogs barking can give a woman a goddamned
migraine headache. And as crazy as this may sound,
every domestic dispute is always the same, only
unique by different names and addresses.

And speaking of addresses, I swear I've been up
in just about every one-, two- and three-bedroom
apartment there is. I've inhaled the various odors
of overflowing trash cans, elevators, dog dung, un-
washed laundry, overused condoms; you name it,
I've smelled it. Just as the air is polluted by noise
and offensive odors, it's also congested with tensions too innumerable to imagine. By the time we
arrive at the scene of a dispute, there's always been
that long history to precede us.

The two contenders had once fallen in love (or
lust) with each other. They found enough interest
between them to want to be closer, so they went
ahead and combined resources. Some got the marriage license; most others didn't, but always the
two somehow found it most convenient to shack up
together. Most times the love brought about children. In many cases there have been children by
other partners, who just happen to be caught up in
the middle of all this bullshit. And there was always pain in these homes. They lived with it now
because they had no other choice. But later on in life
the crap would come back to haunt them. Fatherless

children. Poverty. Maybe drug abuse or overeating. I should know.

Anyhow, in these love nests gone sour, the man and woman (the woman and woman, or the man and man) would inevitably come to find out about each other's glaring faults—the lies and the skeletons that took such intimacy to learn about. This is where, as I said, these squabbles are all the same. One way or the other, someone fell out of love, or out of lust. They changed their minds about the products and services they chose. The bottom line is, they want out and they're willing to go to any means to gain their independence. From there on, it becomes the whole he said, she said mess, and the dishes and drinking glasses start flying. It's the war of the roses and only the strong will survive.

Usually, the weaker party, be it man or woman, is the one to call us. That's when Maritza and I step to the plate. We have our own procedure—oughtta patent it, really—where we separate the two who've been fighting. If the apartment is too small, with no room for privacy, I might take the man out into the hallway. I'm bigger than Maritza (she's just over five feet tall), so it kinda feels natural for me to be the brawn of the dynamic duo. Although that's not to say my girl can't handle her business if it ever goes there. Worse comes to worst, she has the Glock 9, just like me. And damn if she doesn't score a 90 every time we go to the firing range.

These domestic situations can get sticky too, because there's so much glue between the two, whether its money, children or household belongings . . . there's gonna have to be some kind of separation.

Number one, if we even sense that a woman has been beaten by her husband (or her baby's father), out come the handcuffs; nine out of ten times, we're lockin' the guy up. Let them do the explaining in front of the judge. He shoulda kept his hands off of her. Number two, if the two just can't see eye to eye, the man has to be the one to gather his things and step. At that point we inform a domestic counselor in the department about the situation and encourage the woman to file for an order of protection. You never can be too careful in these situations. *Remember O.J.*, we always tell each other, Maritza and I.

Now, if this dispute is one that merely needed Maritza and me to show our faces (and our uniforms) so that one or the other could see that this was serious enough to maybe go to the next level, then we might suggest that the man take a walk. A long walk, during which he might do some thinking—soul-searching, Maritza and I call it, just to make it sound fancy. But always we say, "Now, we don't want to have to come back here again . . . we've got real criminals to chase, you know. If we do come back, somebody's going downtown for somethin' . . . disturbing the peace, attempted assault, endangering the welfare of a

child. Whatever we can think up, ya hear?" And
they always agree. A lot of times, our heavy-
handed way about things is all that was needed to
mend the relationship:

"Okay, so he cheated. That's life. Either she
takes it on the chin and she works to make things
better . . . brush it off and move . . . or else call the
whole thing off. Separate, take him to court, whatever. Maybe you two need to see a marriage counselor. Should I suggest one? But what you don't
wanna do is have us come back here . . ." Or,
"Look at the two beautiful children you both made.
They're more important than anything . . . even
important enough for you two to get over your
petty differences." And so would go our negotia-
tion tactics, with Maritza and I playing Scrabble
with these miserable couples' minds, and then
talking about it while we cruise up and down Webster, Fordham, Jerome and the Grand Concourse.
That was our zone, those four strips of commerce,
of traffic and of tenements. If you began counting
apartment buildings you'd get dizzy before you
reached 200. I swear we're all living and working
like some goddamed sardines in this metal can
known as the Bronx.

IT WAS CLOSE to our one-year anniversary as partners when the call came for a dispute at 1430 Webster Avenue.

"It's the Roses again," I suggested, even without hearing the apartment number or the name of the complaint.

"See a Ms. Robbins . . . apartment 7B," the dispatcher announced.

I looked over at Maritza as I brought the mic to my lips. "That's a ten-four," I responded. Then to my partner I mentioned, "I thought Sonoma got an order of protection."

"She did," Maritza said before she pressed down on the accelerator as if to warn the world we were comin'. Then she thrust the squad car into drive and pulled away from the curb where we had been sitting, watching shoppers with their spring fever (probably both secretly wishing we were amongst them). The gravity from the movement of the vehicle threw me back slightly against the seat. Not a second later, I switched the emergency light.

"Oh boy," I murmured, holding on to an overhead handle. "Somebody's about to get locked up."

With the siren blaring and the emergency lights flashing, Maritza maneuvered the vehicle through traffic, against traffic and practically onto the sidewalk in front of 1430 Webster. There was nothing unusual out here, just some children jumping rope and a local wino ditching his brown bag so that we wouldn't catch him.

Was he kidding?

As expected, the door to the building was busted,

making the buzzer system as irrelevant as a single birth control pill amidst a sea of horny virgins. Nearly out of breath after climbing six flights of stairs to get to the seventh floor (avoiding the wait for the slow-ass elevator), Maritza and I were as upset as two aggravated, overworked officers of the law could be, having to do all that extra stair-climbing to respond to the Robbins call. Again. When we got to the door, I did the knocking.

"Ms. Robbins? Ms. Robbins? Police, Ms. Robbins, open the door." I continued to knock, using the back end of my flashlight, heavy enough to be a weapon itself. Maritza pulled out her baton to help me knock.

After a minute of absolutely dead air, with this and that resident peeking out from their doorways, I gave Maritza this sidelong look. It meant that it was time for more dramatic measures. Both of us stood back. Maritza made a quick radio call to request backup. That was procedure before we kicked in the door. Then I did the honors.

It took three good bangs before the door gave in. We both had our weapons out now, just in case.

"Sonoma? Sonoma?" The two of us crept farther into the apartment, sensing danger with each step. At least I did. You never knew what to expect once you had to take a door down.

We were quiet now, listening for anything that might give us clues as to what was going on. There was a leaking faucet. A television was on, with the theme for *As the World Turns* haunting the atmosphere. This was eerie.

"Sonoma?" We were entering the kitchen now when Maritza shouted, "Sonoma! Shit! Check the fire escape, Sissy!"

This was unreal. Sonoma Robbins was lying on the kitchen floor in a blood-soaked blouse and skirt. Stab wounds were visible in more places that I could count. She was barefoot. Her eyes were looking straight up at the ceiling with tears having already made trails down her cheeks. The woman was in shock, shaking and whimpering from the trauma that her significant other, no doubt, inflicted on her.

"Officer Dickerson! Check the fire escape!" Maritza shouted, but the words were droning echoes in my head. I heard her, but then I didn't. This was like a dream, and I felt myself shaking right in the middle of it. Seconds later I felt a smack against my face. The shock and sting of it shook me, and I suddenly realized that I was in the middle of an emergency.

"Damn it, Sissy! This woman's dying. Help me!" Martiza went back to Sonoma's side and took her head in her hands. "Hold on baby, help's comin'. Hold on."

I immediately radioed for EMS, trying to make up for the lost seconds . . . precious, lost seconds. "Shit!" I cursed myself and rushed to the open window in the kitchen. No sign of anyone on the fire escape. My fault. I squeezed my hand against my face, hoping to rub away this illusion. No, this woman is not gagging there on the floor . . . no she is not coughing up blood . . . no, no, no, this isn't happening.

"Oh, please, Sonoma . . . please hold on," Maritza pleaded there on the kitchen floor, the blood already making its way onto her uniform and bare hands. We're taught to keep a distance from any blood, no matter what. But this was greater than any AIDS scare. This woman was dying here.

Just as I heard sirens advancing toward the building, Maritza let out a scream. That's when my legs buckled and it was lights-out for me. From that moment on, things changed for me. The next thing I remember was an EMS worker with some smelling salts under my nose. Ammonia; whooo-eee! It sure did the trick.

"Officer Dickerson, are you pregnant?" I shook my head. No way. "Allergies?" I shook my head again, not quite there yet with my voice. I couldn't say what I was thinking: I'm allergic to murder. Eventually the EMS worker said it was important for me to be taken to Montefiore Hospital. I'd need a checkup.

There was an oxygen mask over my face before I could protest, and the clean air sent me out of this world. Somewhere in the mist I heard Maritza say, "She'll be okay." But I wanted to know about Sonoma Robbins. No, I didn't. I let my eyelids close. It felt like the thing to do.

I don't know how much time passed between Sonoma Robbins' home and me in the hospital room, but I woke to a pleasant sight. It was my best friend, April Davis.

# APRIL DAVIS

THIS WAS THE second time (so far as I was aware of) that Sissy went into some kind of crazy unconsciousness. To tell the truth, it's making me crazy.

The first time was out in Brooklyn, when that woman got mowed down by a car. When Sissy later explained to me what happened, I couldn't say I blamed her for experiencing that bout of shock. It must've been a horrible sight. I went to be with her in the hours that followed, doing what I could to nurse her back to sanity. I mean, what else are friends for?

And now this.

I stood by Sissy's bedside while a doctor explained what went down. He used some kind of fancy word, but the real deal is that the woman goes into shock when she sees blood. "She just freezes up like a visitor in a haunted house," he told me. I asked the doctor what I could do, and he said to just continue being her friend. He said he wished he had friends as compassionate as me.

I was flattered, but still worried. What would happen to Sissy if she was ever on the job and, God forbid, she saw her partner shot? Blood all over. If she froze up, she wouldn't be able to defend herself. Then I'd lose my best friend. Then I'd be the one at the funeral. Dag. I'd have to have a heart-to-heart talk with Sissy. No question about it.

I MET SISSY Dickerson about a year after she started at the 52nd Precinct. In fact, it wasn't long before the car accident she witnessed. I was on a freelance writing assignment for a feature with *Today's Black Woman* magazine. The publication was concocting themes again—not that concocting themes is so bad, it's just that I'm a realist. I know what makes these things tick.

The theme for this particular issue was Strong Black Women. Not physical might alone, but mental and spiritual might as well. I figured if the magazine was considering personalities of the past and present, they'd be running those same photos again. Oprah, Flo Jo, Harriet Tubman, Tina Turner, Coretta Scott King, and we all know the rest. I was thinking that the assignment should call for more up-to-date personalities. Women who were making moves today. Fresh studies. New faces. So, of course, I had to go and do my thing, like I always do, and submit my own concepts for the theme.

When I heard that Sissy Dickerson was soon to be competing on *Super Woman*, a new reality TV show that had women from all over the country to compete in various triathlon-like activities, I immediately made some calls. April, the investigator. The previews showed Sissy as one of the competitors, and they seemed proud to mention that she was a police officer from the Bronx. Personally, I thought they were happy to add some chocolate to their milk, because most of the other contestants were white or they had some kind of foreign blood in them. Sissy, however, was representing so much more: the Bronx, black women, and police officers throughout the nation. I couldn't let this opportunity get by me.

It was easy to land the interview. Not that the powers that be at the 52nd Precinct made it easy—I had to sit outside of the police station and catch her once her shift was over—but once I did catch up to her she agreed wholeheartedly. The two of us had dinner (my treat) at JP's, that amazing seafood restaurant over on City Island.

We both had drinks to begin with, to lighten up the whole interviewer/interviewee tension that serves as a burdensome barrier on many occasions. Once we got to talking, you couldn't shut us up. It was like . . . well, we had so damned much in common. We were both from the Bronx. Her mother and father divorced when she was five. I told Sissy my circumstances: my father died when I was born, so I never knew him. (As I heard it from my mother, my father didn't get to set his eyes on me outside of the delivery room.) For both Sissy and me, it was like she said about keeping her police partner at a certain emotional distance: you can't miss what you never had.

So when we learned about our fatherlessness, there was that immediate bond. I talked about becoming a born-again Christian and having Jesus to fill my voids. She told me about how her hair began to fall out and how she had an angry teenage life. I talked about pouring myself into my work and being an overachiever. She talked about feeling ugly because of her dark brown skin and nappy hair. Then there was this moment we had where we both cried after I found out that Sissy drew a picture of her father, to the best of her recollection, and posted copies of them around town—HAVE YOU SEEN MY DADDY?—hoping for responses. I, on the other hand, wrote letters and sent birthday cards to my father. They were simply addressed to Dad on the outside the envelope. That was the address—TO DAD. What a mess.

Without the words being said, it was clear to me that Sissy and I had survived years of internal pain and anguish, both of us searching for someone or something to help fill the black hole. Something to help with the issues.

For me it was writing. For Sissy it was the police force. She had that sense of authority to lean on . . . to protect her from the insecurity, the confusion and the sadness that so many women like us experienced.

When the waitress finally came to our table with a tray full of food, her eyes even watered, caught up in the steam of our testimonials. Although I'm sure she did overhear us, it wasn't necessary. Our revelations were airborne for all to absorb.

"I'm surprised you never turned to drugs or alcohol or food," I said to Sissy.

Then she said, "Lucky, I guess. But when I really think about it, work is a drug. And I would enjoy it immensely—is that the word?"

"Immensely is good. Immeasurably is better."

"Okay. So, I would enjoy it immeasurably if the men who are around me would just let me do my job. Why can't they just stay focused? Some of us don't need a man to get by. We don't exactly need a stiff one—excuse my language—"

"Oh, it's okay. It comes with the job."

"Well, then . . . I meant to say, I don't need a hard dick to know my job or to feel secure about myself. I can do just as well with a good book."

"Can I, uh, quote you on that?"

"What the hell . . . it's not like I'm comin' out of the closet or anything, so go ahead. I don't wanna be portrayed as a lesbian or anything like that—don't get me wrong—I just want to be independent. I don't need some sweaty, luggage-toting man to complete me. I got my own luggage. If you feel me."

"Oh, I feel you all right," I told her. I felt comfortable with Sissy now. Like I could ask her almost anything.

"So, it's fair to say you've had a rough childhood and that you've grown up to be an I-don't-take-no-mess kind of woman."

"Exactly," Sissy replied.

"Is that the kind of tough-mindedness that makes you a strong black woman?"

"Maybe. But maybe it's about color, too. I ain't no fool. I know that television has to be politically correct nowadays."

"I'm glad you said that, Sissy. Because I'm feeling you as a representative of sorts. Of our culture, of a woman's endurance. Of police officers! Oh! You're reppin' the Bronx, too!" I wanted to tell her more, but I held it in.

"The Boogie-down, baby."

"So, now, addressing the *Super Woman* gig . . . are you prepared for this Rambo stuff they're bound to put you through? I heard there's mud wrestling, tree climbing and—do I have it right? You all have to swim through a pool filled with Jell-O? Actual Jell-O? The kind you eat?

"Actual Jell-O. The kind you eat. And you know this is all sexist shit; excuse my French again, but we're supposed to do this in two-piece bathing suits, no caps, no goggles . . . I mean, this is gonna be really slimy."

"It sounds like it," I said.

Sissy and I talked while we ate, leaving me little opportunity to buckle down with the whole pad and pen bit. But I was so immersed in the conversation . . . mental images were, like, tattooed on my cranium walls. How could I ever forget what I would inevitably see on national television? Mud wresting, tree climbing, swimming in Jell-O? Wow. I have to say, it did sound a bit . . . exciting? Note to self: must have my head checked. I also hoped deep down that Sissy beat those other women. As far as I was concerned, she was also representing me. My hero, Sissy Dickerson, Superwoman. Go Sissy!

TWO WEEKS AFTER I held the interview, the editors at *Today's Black Woman* accepted my story about Sissy. They already had stories about a Super Diva (some new singer/songwriter/producer) who was now stepping into the acting world. There was a story about a Superhero (a fire fighter) who on three different occasions ran into burning flames to rescue people and pets. There was also a story about a Super Leader (an activist) who spearheaded an all-female march to protest job discrimination in various epicenters around the country. The effort resulted in a new law that not only would enforce more than merely fundamental rights, but would also address some of the hidden tactics that nurtured the imbalance between the haves and the have-nots.

My story painted Sissy Dickerson as Super-woman, which went so well with the Strong Black Woman theme that *Today's Black Woman* wanted, but it was also like knocking out two birds with one stone, since it helped to promote the television show itself. So, me being the intelligent woman that I am, I addressed the producers of the television show, explaining that I had a confirmed publishing date for my story. I also showed them how I would be assisting them in their marketing efforts. Putting that whole "Superwoman" thing out there in front of a few million more faces would, in fact, boost their ratings for the show, considering how many is-sues of *Today's Black Woman* would be printed.

In the end, I convinced the producers that my efforts were worth a few bucks. They agreed and sent me a check for $2,500. I thought that my work was worth two or three times that, but I was con-tent with covering a month's rent and a few other bills. Mo' money, mo' money, mo' money!

The *Today's Black Woman* issue hit stands just weeks before the show aired. Sissy gave me a call, thanking me and asking me to wish her luck. But I said, "I'll do you one better, girlfriend. I'll pray for you."

"I guess it don't get no better than that," Sissy said.

"I really hope to see you again, April. I don't re-ally have too many friends, ya know?"

"I'm feelin' you, Sissy. We'll do lunch real soon."

And then we hung up. But deep down I had some kinda love for the warm feeling that followed the call. God would forgive me.

The night of the *Super Woman* show, I made a bowl of popcorn for me and Coco Puff to enjoy. Coco Puff is Sissy's pit bull. He stayed over while Sissy was in L.A.

"That's her, Coco Puff! Go Sissy!" I munched down my popcorn like it was a juicy steak, like I was a woman who hadn't eaten in days. "Oh my GOD!" I cried out.

Sissy and some woman named Mad Marsha were scrambling in the mud. The Amazon woman grabbed Sissy's breast from behind. I could almost feel it myself, how Mad Marsha clenched the breast like it was a water balloons barely withstanding the pressure.

"Good! Yeah!" I yelled when Sissy stomped Mad Marsha's foot. Then she gave the large woman an elbow to the gut. "Yes! Yes-yes-yes!" I winced after I said that, knowing that there was something very ungodly about rooting for this kind of violence, especially when I knew it wasn't pretend. "What're you lookin' at?" I said to Coco Puff and he turned back to the television.

Sissy flipped Mad Marsha onto her back and then jumped down onto her for a three-count. I screamed with pride. "That's my girl! Go Sissy!"

The commercials came on after an announcer promised "more wrestling after these messages." It seemed as though there was to be a process of elimination.

I took a special interest in the other contenders, checking for any illegal moves that they might make and hoping that Sissy would be just as alert. Sissy's elbowing and foot stomping were just as illegal, but the referee hadn't seen those acts. And besides, the way Mad Marsha grabbed Sissy's breast was dead wrong. So, good for her that they had to take her away on the stretcher.

I sat through two more matches before the semifinals. Some woman with a flat chest and pigtails was battling a bald-headed chubby woman with a big ole wart on her nose. Pigtails won the match and waited to see who the victor was between Sissy and the Bride of Frankenstein—an extremely light-skinned woman whose makeup was all wrong; nothing could hide that four-inch scar across her cheek. I wondered where they dug up these women from.

"Come on, Sissy . . . you can do it, baby!"

These two stood facing one another, readying themselves in horse stances more or less listening to the referee spit the rules of the match. A whistle finally blew and the two went at it. They circled each other, their bare feet stomping through the wet, soupy mud, their hands reaching out for a grab here and there. Nobody got a grip.

"Oh shit!" I exclaimed. My hand went to my

mouth. Coco Puff turned to look at me like I'd suddenly caught on fire. But I was actually choking on popcorn. Sissy! She reached out and smacked the scar-faced woman. The vulgarity from my lips was an uncontrollable reflex that I couldn't seem to avoid. I immediately dropped down to my knees and turned my back to the television, folding my hands and bowing my head in prayer over the couch.

"Jesus, forgive me for I have sinned..." I squeezed my eyes closed as I sought forgiveness. There was excitement on the television screen behind me, but Sissy could handle herself. I had to repent. Coco Puff barked at the screen. A minute later I turned around to find that Sissy had won the semifinal. Thank God.

Commercials came on and I could only imagine what would go down in the finals.

# RIVER

NICKY WAS A player, and I knew this going in. So it made what I was about to do to him A-OK. He said he was single, but I found out he had women all over New York begging for his attention. All because he rode in the passenger seat of some multi-platinum rapper.

He said he had a six-figure publishing deal with Universal Records. But that was a damned lie. He wasn't doin' nothin but feeding off of his sidekick status. There was no such publishing deal, with Universal or any other major record company. Finally, I found out that Nicky liked to mess with young girls—as young as fifteen or sixteen, and naive to the ways of the player, falling heavy for Nicky's proclaimed status. But Nicky's game was to make promises that were the furthest from the truth, pipe dreams at best. And he'd talk it up enough, until he got to the bedroom, the dressing room, the hotel room, and even the tour bus. Any of those spots were perfect to finish up with the groupie of the day.

Long story short, Pretty Nicky's game finally came to an end once he met me. I must've been looking particularly delicious for him to wanna hit on me that night at The Ritz. I was minding my own business, having a rum and coke at the bar, when he stepped to me. I gave him my best "nigga, please" expression, but he kept tryin'. I appreciate that in a man, his relentless ways. Maybe a little arrogance. But go too far and you might get hurt like so many others have. The body count is now 18, to be exact.

Nicky (number 19) was very fit, about six feet tall, with a shaved head, a nice round ass and the cutest baby face. Now that I think of it, he could have been a church boy who happened to grow up in a callous world, adopting that thug-like presence in order to hide everything else he was lacking. But I saw beyond the mask. Eventually, I was able to convince him to join me for a one-night stand. We went to a seedy hotel just off of the thruway, and before you know it, Nicky was putting it in my ass doggy-style. I could have been a normal woman and indulged in simple sex, but I told him I was on my period and then said, "Call it what you want, but you are not gonna stick your dick in my bloody walls."

The fact of the matter is, the man fucked me like

a champ. Only, I came early. And then I screamed for him to take it out. Nothin' more painful or irritating than getting fucked when you're not excited. Just when I thought Nicky was obeying me, he forced himself where I told him not to go. I had lied about being on my period, and now he too realized that I lied.

The bizarre acts that followed should be noted somewhere in a warning manual for potential rape victims, i.e., every woman. He smacked my ass and it hurt like he was using a leather whip. I whimpered as he overpowered me. He covered my mouth with his palm.

"Sorry, baby. I paid good money for this, and I want what's comin' to me!" Nicky drove himself into me again and again. I was wet enough to receive him without tearing, so things weren't as bad as they could've been. However, rape is rape. Whatever I didn't want, for whatever reason, was my decision. Not his to take as he pleased. Bottom line: I didn't want him in my pussy. When Nicky finally busted off inside of me, he broke down and cried.

Oh, shit! This mothafucka's a straight wacko!

"I'm sorry, River. I let myself get out of hand. I didn't mean it. I . . . I swear I'm sorry, baby. Will you forgive me?" Nicky pleaded.

"Forgive you? Nicky, relax. It's okay, really. That was the best fuck I ever had. Against my will . . . plus you ran up in me like a garden hose.

Oh God! That was good." And I kissed Nicky's open mouth.

"Here, baby . . . lemme take care of that little friend." I nibbled my way down Nicky's chest, his stomach and took his grimy, limp penis in my mouth. Just to taste myself was pleasurable enough, but in the meantime I had this jerk fooled. He was probably thinkin' of me as the freakiest bitch he ever took to bed. No doubt, he'd want me back again. And I smiled to myself, knowing that Sally was close by, and that I could fuck this guy up without thinkin' twice. But the motel people saw me, the bartender at the Ritz saw us talking . . . served us drinks. My fingerprints were probably everywhere. Oh no, now wasn't the time. But the time would definitely come. Nicky was surely gonna get his.

For weeks I ignored Nicky's calls, knowing that there would be greater anticipation with each moment. He was desperate for some more of this freak. Then, finally, I called him back.

"Damn, baby! What the fuck—where you been? I've been trying to get back wit'cha for weeks."

"Oh . . . I . . . I wasn't sure you really wanted me," I told him.

"You weren't sure? You weren't sure? Does a fish need water? Does the earth need the sun? Baby, I need you like I need oxygen! Can I see you now?"

I thought about it. Okay, buddy, but this has gotta play out *my* way.

I told him, "Tonight. Meet me by the Fordham Road entrance to the Bronx Zoo."

"The Bronx Zoo? Tonight? Don't they close at a certain time?"

"Listen, if you don't wanna do this, I'll understand. I just had something, well, special in mind." Special. Come on, asshole. Read between the lines here. Special means freaky!

"Special, huh? Mmm . . . what time can we do this, uhh, special thing?"

"How about midnight?"

"Okay," he replied, more insecurity than ever in his voice. "If you say so, baby."

"I say so. Oh . . . and I need you to bring along a tub of butter with you. Stop by Pathmark or C-Town to get it."

"A tub of butter? Well . . . what'd you have in mind?"

"You'll just have to wait 'n see, playboy. Now don't let me down," I told him. Then I hung up before another word was spoken.

I'LL NEVER FORGET that day. It was the second Wednesday in June, and midnight was fast approaching as I stood in the parking lot at the Bronx Zoo. This was such a pleasant evening, so perfect for the fun I had planned for Nicky and me. The fun was about to begin once Nicky's Lexus swung into the empty lot. The headlights were bright enough that I had to squint as he came closer, stopping the car just a few feet from me, leaving his headlights on to illuminate me as well as the zoo's entrance behind me.

I stepped up to the car, put my hands on the warm hood and got all sexy with my pursed lips and enough cleavage showing to border on indecent exposure. I blew Nicky a kiss and he quickly jumped out of the car. "Shut the engine down, baby. You'll wake the animals."

Nicky made a strange face, but he did as I asked. Then he came around to where I was leaning against his sleeping headlights.

"Now, what's all this about, baby?" Nicky bent in for a kiss on his approach, but I saw it coming and made the first move; just a peck on his cheek. I hugged him as well, to keep him from wanting a deeper kiss, making sure to brush his silk-shirted chest with my breasts. I hope he feels how hard my nipples are, I thought.

"Come with me, boo. And bring the butter," I said. I knew he was watching as I swung my ass and pivoted off toward the entrance gate. I heard frenzied movement as Nicky got the butter and as he hurried to catch up with me. The zoo has a box office out front, which had closed shutters and signage to show the various prices for admission.

A seaweed green wrought-iron gate encloses the zoo itself, stretching for miles around the entire park. If I didn't know any better, I'd assume that this was a prison for both wild and tamed animals.

The fact that it was smack-dab in the middle of the Bronx was irrelevant. A lock, a fence, a cage . . . it all amounts to prison.

"Where'd you get that?" Nicky asked, as I held up the key to the gate.

"I have friends in high places," I announced, trying to be vague. "The key to the park? Shit. You must know the zookeeper or something."

"He's my daddy," I lied. Then I pushed open the gate and stepped in. "Comin'?"

Bewildered, Nicky followed me in. I locked the gate behind us. While the moon's glow enabled us to see our way along the path, Nicky and I held hands like newlyweds strolling along lovers' lane.

"So, you been thinkin about me, Nicky?"

"Have I? I wanna marry your pretty ass!"

"You think I'm pretty?"

"The prettiest."

"If I let you have it tonight do you promise to do me like you did before? Will you treat me like a bad girl? Will you punish me?"

"Ooooh . . . your wish is my command, baby."

Ten minutes into our walk, we had already passed the children's zoo, the rhinoceroses, giraffes, rams, elephants and zebras. Of course they were asleep in their respective areas, but we could still see their rested bodies in the distance.

"I always wondered why the apes just don't break out and escape," I mentioned. "I mean, they're strong enough, smart enough and they can definitely climb their asses off."

"Yeah, but maybe they're smart enough to know that once they do escape and maybe kill some-body, their ass is grass."

"Like King Kong," I suggested. "Yup. If an ape ever saw that movie, they'd keep their asses put. Now . . . baby, can you tell me what were doin' in here? The anticipation is driving me crazy." Nicky was anxious now.

"Just a little more, boo . . . I have a surprise for you." We were passing The World of Reptiles now.

"A surprise that has something to do with sex?"

"Oh, of course! What else?" Nicky made an ex-haustive sound. He said, "You are one—freaky—bitch."

"Mmm-hmm . . . and you're gonna love every minute of me," I said, squeezing his ass for en-couragement. Another path brought us to where I wanted to be.

"Another key? Damn, baby, your pop's really does run this place, doesn't he?"

I smiled a wicked smile and told Nicky to fol-low me. We were now inside the building known as the House of Cats. "Now, this is incredible," Nicky said as we progressed along an indoor walkway. Glass-enclosed exhibits with dim lighting were to our left and right, stretching for nearly a block. I switched on the lights and a confusion of cat cries roared behind the glass. The exhibits were set up to resemble caves and cliffs and ponds, all of it safe from public access. Nicky was still out in front of me, mesmerized by what he saw.

In the meantime, the wildlife that seemed just out of reach was stirring with rage. We had wakened them. But of course this was nothing new to me; the panthers, cheetahs, bobcats, lions and tigers . . . a jaguar with a brownish-yellow coat prowled across a large tree stump; he peered out occasionally to the public viewing area, as though calculating, plotting or preying.

Another exhibit came to life with cubs, one rolling on its back, another engaging in a suddenly restless bout with its equal. This was once my sanctuary as much as it was theirs. I spent many hours here as a tour guide in the House of Cats. I knew that to interrupt their sleep was lethal. I also knew that they would gladly help me with getting rid of Nicky.

"See those twin lions up there, Nicky?"

"Yeah! And they sure can see me, too."

"Well, those are two of the most dangerous African beasts on the planet. They're from India, you know . . . they once ruled the jungle. Absolute royalty . . ."

"What, did your father school you on all this stuff? River, the lion queen?"

Nicky thought he was witty, I guess. And I laughed—at him, not with him. Still, he had no idea what I had in store.

"No . . . not quite, Nicky. See . . . my father doesn't really run this place. And the key? Well, the truth is I made copies for myself . . ." I was a safe distance from Nicky, halfway along the corridor where public viewing took place during the days. No one, but no one was permitted in here at night. I also knew that park security made rounds along the perimeter at two-hour intervals. I figured by now they'd probably spotted Nicky's car, so I didn't have too much time to play games. There were one or two other guards inside the park, but they mostly slept through their shifts; at least that was what Brad told me when I was sleeping with him. We're not sleeping together anymore. To be blunt about it, Brad's not sleeping with anyone anymore.

"See . . . I used to work here. So I know how this place operates. Plus, I used to fuck one of the guards . . ." I sighed and wagged my head. The naked truth . . . what a thrill it is to tell.

"Poor Brad. It was nice while it lasted . . ." As I said this, I had warm recollections of how I brought Brad into the House of Cats months ago. Only, that was an idea that we both agreed on. Not this time. What Nicky was now experiencing was original. I went into my purse for Sally.

"Oh God, no!"

"No sense yelling, Nicky. Nobody can hear you. It's just you and me inside of a hundred acres of zoo. You . . . me . . . and those twins up there. Those hungry twins."

"River! What's gotten into you? What's this about? Why the gun?"

"It's about you hurtin' me. It's about you takin' advantage of young women. Girls. It's about you lyin' to get your way . . . take off your clothes—we've had enough talk."

Nicky was still. He didn't budge. So I raised the gun and squeezed off a shot. The bullet ricocheted off the cement floor and caused Nicky to drop the butter.

"River!" he yelled, dancing as if to avoid the bullet.

But I didn't want to shoot Nicky. I wanted to see a show. A vicious, nutritious show.

"Now, either you get your clothes off, or I'ma make you look like holy hell. Very holey." Nicky began to undress. "Too slow playboy," I said. So he stepped up the pace. "See, it's dogs like you that make life painful for women. You get your shit off for five seconds . . . have your goddamed way with us, spray your venom in our faces, into our temples . . . but we have to live with your quick thrill for our entire lives."

"But, River . . ." Nicky was crying now; the tears wet his naked chest. "I never—"

"But, River, nothin'. Scoop some of that butter in your hands. A lot of it. Now!" Nicky did just as I asked. Naked fool. "Now start spreadin' it on your body. I'm gonna make sure this meal is nice and tasty."

"Fuck this!" Nicky said. He stomped his bare foot and threw down the globs of butter he had scooped up. "You're just gonna have to shoot me!"

Maybe he thought I was joking, but I went ahead and did as he asked. I pointed Sally at Nicky's foot and I pulled the trigger. He fell, holding his foot for dear life while he screamed bloody murder.

Little did he know how easy that was for me. Easy, and pleasurable, besides.

"Now, again: scoop some goddamned butter, and put it on your body."

Nicky whimpered and snorted to the point that I almost felt sorry for him. He looked like a fuckin' kid there on the floor; a kid crying after a hardass-whuppin'. Bloody foot and all, Nicky got up from the floor and did his best to bend down for the butter.

"Nicky, Nicky, Nicky—tsk, tsk, tsk—get up. Get—up!" I moved close enough to poke the muzzle of the gun at his forehead. "You don't wanna fuck with a woman who has issues," I told him. He was shaking, pretending. Wearing a mask. Just like they all do. Fakes, phonies and frauds. "The butter. Now." Nicky began to baste himself, rubbing the yellow gunk about his chest and arms. I love it when a plan comes together.

"All over. Make sure you get the dick and balls, too . . . Now the legs . . . keep going, ankles. Now put some on that bald head of yours. You think you can fool me by shaving your head? I know you lost some hair up there, you forty-year-old fool." Nicky looked surprised that I had seen through his charade.

"What? A black woman can't do her homework? I know all about you. Couldn't get a real job, so you went for the ride with your rapper friends, perpetratin'. Well, those days are over. Walk." I indicated for him to move further down the corridor. I could sense the hunger of the wild cats as we passed their man-made habitats. Their wild cries built up to an orchestral threat.

Toward the rear of the exhibits was a short turn and a doorway where attendants usually fed the cats. Sally and I urged Nicky to step aside while we fired at the padlock.

"Take off the chain and go in." Nicky stood shivering. He had to know that this was it. That this was how he would die.

"River . . . p-p-please don't d-d-do th-th-this. Please."

"Too late for plea bargains. You shoulda thought about that when you raped me."

"B-but I didn't rape you! You said you liked it!"

"I lied," I said. Then I fired another shot between Nicky's legs. He began to urinate on himself. And I got to laughing again. "Poor, poor Nicky . . . can't even hold your water in!"

Once Nicky was over the threshold, I reached for the door to close it. "A word to the wise, baby . . . run!" I advised him as I shut the door. Nicky was banging on the opposite side of the glass, making a whole lot of noise, yelling and whatnot. I knew that this would do nothing less than speed up the process.

I stepped back around to the viewing area where I could see through the glass-enclosed exhibit. Nicky was crouched in a corner and the twins, Kuno and Kimba, rose up from their resting places. The beasts were as big as Cadillacs, now creeping down from the short cliff, zeroing in on their butter-basted meal. When he was within reach, Kuno casually stretched out his paw in what might have appeared to be a playful way. But I knew that those claws of his (and hers) were deadly. Now Kimba crept closer, appraising her prey, sweeping a paw across the front of Nicky.

At first, I thought it was another playful stroke, but a second look told me the feast had started. Kimba's sharp claws sliced Nicky's buttery thigh with three deep, bloody wounds. I felt my insides quiver with delight as Nicky's hell-raising cry filled the House of Cats.

The lions had stayed at a safe distance, enough to taste-test their victim. When they realized that Nicky was no real threat, they advanced on him, tackled him flat. They each mauled the body from both sides, sinking their teeth into the flesh of the throat, the thigh, the gut. Nicky shook and convulsed for a moment; something like a helpless seizure victim, until he was no more than a lifeless, bloody mess.

I too shivered as sensations of the events before me shot up from my moist folds to my chest, then taking my mind by storm. I couldn't imagine that this latest encounter would give me that same high as before, but it did. I held onto the brass handrail, frozen with my own rapture, and continued to look on with guilty pleasure. My breath fogged part of the view as I became weak, my head against the glass. Meanwhile, the lions lay with that fresh kill between their paws, lapping at the juice, chomping at the white meat. Other cats roared and caused commotion in their jealous rage over the unshared steak.

It all began to fade into a kind of dream for me; the cats eating a man alive, while others served as a sort of outraged audience. In time, I regained enough of my composure to erase my marks from the glass. Then I let myself out through an exit at the opposite end of the park. It was weird, but I felt like a spent woman after a long, thorough fuck. I was totally satisfied.

# SISSY

I MUST'VE EARNED a lot of brownie points after that *Super Woman* show. I didn't come in first place, but second place apparently brought some credibility with it.

April and I planned a little celebration when I came home from L.A. Just somethin' between the two of us. I thought about inviting Maritza, but there was this unspoken don't-get-too-friendly cloud hanging over our heads. The crazy thing is, I am aware of this stupid rule, and I still feed into it like a damn fool. Oh well. At least I know we'll be on our jobs if worse comes to worst. We won't be thinking like friends, but police officers. I guess.

"Everybody's proud of you on the force," April said while we shopped for our first pig-out party together.

"How do you know?" I asked.

"Well . . . I didn't tell you this, but I thought I'd do a follow-up story—you never know, it could lead to other things."

"Like?" I asked.

"Well, I remember after that woman won on *Survivor* how she did all those interviews: *Good Morning America*, E!, *Entertainment Tonight*. You know, the usual Hollywood circuit. She even had movie offers 'nstuff."

"But she was a winner, April. This country isn't interested in second-place people. They want first-place folks with both their eyes, their legs and a good dental plan. This way, when a first-place person has a dilemma or problems in their lives, the media can hurt and prey on and slaughter them. It's like being fed to the lions."

"So you'd rather be a second-place winner?"

"If it's to keep my sanity, hell yeah. They can have their Hollywood girls, all perfect and saditty. Who wants a dark-skinned woman with nappy hair and dick-suckin' lips anyway?"

April sucked her teeth. "Now, where did you get that from? Your lips are not—well . . . they're not what you said. They're just fine."

"So you say. But your opinion is biased, April."

"How so?" April removed her eyeglasses, lookin' all serious.

"Uh . . . it could have something to do with your lips, baby. If you haven't noticed, they're not too much different than mine."

"Okay . . . but because I have full lips doesn't have to mean . . . well, you know. What you said."

"See, there you go, gettin' all church-like and religious again. Girl, you tellin' me you never sucked a dick before?"

"Sissy! I'm a born-again Christian! I don't speak that way. And I definitely don't think that way." April folded her arms and scowled at me.

"Born-again. Huh! You ain't convincin' me that because you was born-again yesterday that you weren't freakin' the day before. Psssh . . . every girl got some freak in her, so don't even try to deny it."

April started singin',

> *"Jesus loves me, this I know,*
> *For the Bible tells me so . . ."*

So I made up my own song to compete with hers:

> *"Dick-suckin' lips,*
> *Baby-makin hips,*
> *Dick-suckin' lips,*
> *Baby, work that clit!"*

Then she got louder.

> *"Little ones to Him belong,*
> *They are weak but He is strong . . ."*

So I got louder, too.

> *"Dick-suckin' lips!*
> *Dick-suckin' lips!*

*April Davis got dick-suckin' lips!"*
*"Yes! Jesus loves me!*
*Yes! Jesus loves me!"*

We were goin' back and forth, now. But because we were so damned loud, I'm sure that she couldn't hear me. I know I couldn't hear her, as loud as my mouth is.

> *"You can't deny it,*
> *Don't even try it,*
> *You got dick-suckin' lips like me,*
> *You got a diamond-studded clit*
>     *like me!"*

"Yes! Jesus! Loves! Me! The Bible tells me sooooo!" April shouted.

"Freak-a-the week!" I responded louder.

"Stop it! Stop it! Stop it!" April put her hands over her ears and squeezed her eyes shut as she shouted, trying to block me out. I'm sure I was driving her as crazy as she was me.

That was when we heard a knock at the door. We both froze and swung our heads toward the front door, then back toward each other.

"Who could that be?" I wondered out loud.

"Maybe it's the neighbors," April suggested. "Maybe we woke them." But it was only 10 P.M.

"We, nothin'. You're the one who screamed," I insisted.

"So, sue me," April replied.

"Who is it?" I asked when I got near the door, suddenly feeling vulnerable without the Glock on my hip.

"Sissy Dickerson?" a voice inquired.

"Who wants to know?" I asked. When the answer didn't come, I checked the peephole. But nobody was out there.

"What?" April asked.

"I must be hearin' things. You heard the knock and the man's voice, right?"

"Of course," answered April.

"Get back away from the door," I told my houseguest. Then I went for my gun and turned off the lights. You never could be too safe in the Bronx. Especially two black women partying alone.

"Now, I'm gonna ask you again. Who is it?!" I said this loud enough for whoever was outside my door to hear. In the meantime, I had my piece raised. As I turned the doorknob, I hoped he wouldn't see me as just another woman. As if I couldn't shoot straight. April gasped when she realized what I was about to do.

"Back, April," I insisted in a low voice. Then I pulled the door open, expecting to see someone. Anyone. I was ready for the challenge.

April saw it first. "Sissy, down there. The basket."

"Oh," I said. And I looked out into the hallway. Nobody in sight. The presumed danger quickly faded away. I looked back at April with a shrug before I said, "You never can be too careful, girl. You know the city goes into high alert every time the higher-ups get a hard-on. Makes everybody all tense; especially a cop who's on her period . . .

"Now what?" I said as I bent down to pick up a bassinet-size wicker basket filled with fruit, fine champagne, wine and a bouquet of flowers.

"Wow . . . seems like somebody's interested in what he sees."

I closed the door and turned on my house lights again. Then I placed the generous gift on my coffee table. April and I sat on the couch, the excitement and curiosity washing away all evidence of the intense squabble we had minutes earlier. I unfolded the note that came with the gift.

FROM YOUR SECRET ADMIRER.
CONGRATULATIONS, SUPERWOMAN.
YOU'LL ALWAYS BE #1 IN MY HEART.

April leaned closer to see. "Who is it?"
"Beats me."
"I told you. They're proud of you at the 52nd."
"Vapors, baby. Don't let 'em fool you."
"Vapors?"
"Mmm-hmm . . . what was it that rapper said? 'Everybody wants to know when you're on top . . . nobody comes around when your star starts to drop.'"

April took a deep breath and released an exhaustive sigh. Maybe she didn't get it. "Well, Sissy . . . I suppose it's the thought that counts."

"Yeah. And right now, I feel like drinkin'," I said as we set ourselves up for a toast.

"But don't get crazy with it. You've got work to think of."

"Are you kiddin'?" I said to her. "Remember? They simply love me at the job! I'll just call in sick, baby. In the meantime . . . let's you and I drink. To superwomen."

"And secret admirers," April added. And we raised our glasses.

THIS WASN'T THE last basket of cheer I received. I got one after the incident with Sonoma Robbins, not that her murder was anything to celebrate. But the note said, "Just a little something to lift your spirits," and was signed "S. A." From secret admirer. And it did lift my spirits, to the point that I finished that entire bottle of Moët all by my lonesome. Some things didn't require best friends.

There was one other surprise basket. And this time I knew it had to be from somebody at work. Not because of the twelve white roses, the expensive champagne or the idea that some man knew my home address. No. This one had a note to say, "Congratulations on 2 years with the 52nd. Keep up the good work. S. A."

Okay. So I considered the different people who might know how long I'd been with the Bronx precinct. The suspense and all of this sneaking up to my apartment door was driving me insane. I called April about it.

"Guess what . . . I received another basket."

"Mister S.A. again? Did you get a look at him yet?"

"No. The basket was by my door when I got home from work."

"So, what's the occasion this time?" I read the note over the phone. April said, "Two years? Has it been that long?"

"It feels like ten years, for real."

"How do you mean?"

"The streets, April. The violence, the confusion, the never-ending misery . . . it's all beginning to tax me. I thought that coming out here would make a difference."

"You're still upset about Sonoma Robbins, aren't you?"

"Maybe. I still can't believe they let him go, April. How he killed that woman . . . it was so obvious . . . and they had a track record of disputes."

"Can I come over and help you celebrate, sista-friend?"

"I'd like that," I told her.

APRIL AND I got to drinking, talking and forming our own opinions. It seemed we could never run out of topics.

"You can't let yourself get all fired up about it,

Sissy. This is like a pattern that reaches as far back as Cleopatra. Maybe as far back as Eve! I mean, I was skipping through the channels the other day and I stopped to see this black-and-white movie— and you know with all the color on the television these days, to get me to watch a black-and-white flick takes a lot. Anyhow, this was dated back in the fifties and it looked like it was an up-north film (as opposed to a waaay down south, cotton-pickin' setting). Let's just say it took place in . . . Virginia."

"That's up north?" I asked, thinking April had lost her marbles.

"It's more up north than, say, Alabama."

"True."

"But let me get to the story. It was about a couple. The wife was played by that singer, Abbey Lincoln. The husband was some nobody who I never heard of. I mean, he wasn't any Paul Robeson or Sidney Poitier, but he was as black as shoe polish, girl. I mean, black like midnight with no moon."

"What's that gotta do with—"

"She was light skinned. Red bone . . ."

"Okay."

"And, well, that's really the juice of the story. She had a more privileged background than him. I remember one of his lines where he said, 'you ain't never known what it's like to be no nigger.' But that wasn't the hard part for me, Sissy. What hurt was the ignorance of the husband, and even the racist whites who triggered these feelings in the first place. It hurt that the woman didn't have a voice. She couldn't respond, or wasn't given a script that could answer back to the verbal or physical violence, or the racism. It was one thing not to be able to understand what was happening to them, but it was another not to be able to say anything."

"That shit wouldn't happen to me. I'd pop a hot one in any man the minute he laid hands on me."

April sucked her teeth and said, "Girl, they didn't even have female cops back then, much less black female cops. But that's not even the issue here. Yes, there was, and is, inequality. Yes, dark-skinned and light-skinned blacks can't get along, and yes, all of us have experienced racism from then until now. However, black women, Sissy, have been enduring the worst of it all. We get to cope with all the world's immaturity, plus we serve as the sounding board, the punching bag, the latex condom and the safety net for the black man."

"You don't have to tell me that. I'm the one these same women call, at least here in the 52nd Precinct, when they man whups on 'em. You know they assigned me as Maritza's partner for good, right?"

"No. I didn't. You've told me things here and there, but—"

"Well, lemme tell you, chile. That's our thing. Domestic disturbances and domestic violence. We know how to handle these couples and their issues. Got it down to a science. I've seen more bruises and heard more excuses than on a whole season of *COPS*."

"And that's just what I'm talkin' about, Sissy. This horrendous, vicious pattern. If you're seeing all of this here in the Bronx, imagine how much of it is going on in some small town, somewhere where the cops just say, 'Y'all betta git yer act together,' then turn their back," April said.

To that, I added, "And as soon as they're behind that closed door, the beat down starts up all over again."

"So that's why you can't let it get to you, Sissy. You can't let it corrupt your mind. If you do, you'll never find a husband."

I laughed aloud. "Ha! Who wants a husband? I told you, girlfriend. Sperm donor. Nothing more, nothing less."

"Yeah. And then your daughter grows up like you and me."

"What's so bad about that? We're healthy."

"But without fathers," April said. And that comment called for another glass of bubbly. For the rest of the night, April and I drank until we cried.

# APRIL

I HAD BEEN writing special interest stories that were so interesting and uncommon they could've published themselves in women's magazines and in the lifestyle sections of some select newspapers. Ultimately, I was pigeonholing myself as the kind of writer who got beneath the skin of her subjects. I was a writer who could show what a woman was really made of. But despite our depth, and despite our many dimensions, the need for such female-centered stories was limited and could only bring in so much money.

They say that in a world full of colors, we can choose what colors we'd like to focus on. And maybe all this time I was focusing on mint green. No—more like olive green. Not too much of that out there; a color that you'd be hard-pressed to find in an average Crayola box. But all the while, red was in heavy demand. Where olive green was lifestyle stories, red was the sex and violence. My bills called for the kind of money that red-hot sex and violence could attract.

I decided to make some moves. I planned to mine some of Sissy's stories. She rarely speaks about her police work, but she said something about this one case the night we got filthy drunk. At the time, I was too sick to ask her more about it. But the idea of a killer on the loose in the Bronx has been like a tumor in the back of my mind, just growing and throbbing with every passing minute. I mean, heck, if there's a killer on the loose, how safe could I be?

My other idea is a secret. I wouldn't dare tell Sissy about, or anybody else. I'm thinking of doing something less than godly. I'm thinking of writing romance novels under another name. Perhaps something like Tuesday for a first name and Mourning as my last. It's catchy: *"Did you read that bestseller written by Tuesday?" "Tuesday who?" "Tuesday Mourning, that's who."* It has a nice ring to it.

My only problem with the romance novel idea is that in this day and age you've gotta be raunchy to make money. Otherwise, you have to be incredibly talented, to the degree that folks would feel as though they absolutely had to buy your book. It's a scary choice, but I'll have to pray on it. Raunch might sell, but not for a woman of God.

And one other thing. I wondered if I could get closer to Sissy, if maybe I could interview some of these abused women. I could investigate and expose these men for the monsters they are. Maybe I could get the *Daily News* to buy the idea, to print pictures, names, addresses . . . all that. Just like they do with child molesters. If not the *Daily News,* perhaps some local paper in Long Island or Westchester would go for the idea. To have the idea in a smaller paper might add credibility; it could even serve as a sort of endorsement. And then I could take that whole project to the *Daily News* and say, See? I came to you first with this idea, and now look what these other papers have. A winner. Then, of course, I'd talk the editor into going along with it. People always like to believe they can get a hold of a good idea.

That bit was on the back burner of my mind for now. First things first. I'd have to make my move on this Bronx killer that Sissy talks about. She says she's sure it's a serial killer that's doing this and I remember seeing a story on the six o'clock news about the Pink Heart murders. So I put two and two together, and I figured that must be the case she was blabbering about. The only thing is, I couldn't imagine why this one would bother her. After all, she wasn't a detective or anything. All she did was drive around with Maritza Garcia on the domestic disturbance tour. So why the mention about this killer on the loose? What was it to her? Where was the connection?

ONE EVENING I thought I'd surprise Sissy. I shopped for dinner and went to her house to prepare a

home-cooked meal. Sissy loves my barbecued
chicken, so I knew that she'd be grateful to arrive
home from work, exhausted and hungry, suddenly
facing my feast. Afterward, we'd talk, heart to
heart.

I have the key to Sissy's apartment, as she does
mine, for emergency purposes. (We single women
have got to stick together.) The only worry I had
was Coco Puff, Sissy's pit bull. Oh, Coco Puff is
friendly to me all the time, always kissing my hand
when I visit Sissy. And Coco Puff is a female pit
bull! I don't think I've ever been so close to a female pit bull; or any pit bull, for that matter. The
thing I was concerned about was, what if the pit
bull hadn't been fed? I could be her next meal. I
took the chance anyhow. Shoot, I had a hungry
woman to cook for.

When I got to Sissy's place, I was surprised to
see an older man by her door. I could see that he
had been crouched by her welcome mat, and a
closer look made me gasp. It's him! The man had
to be at least forty-nine. He was clean-shaven and
had a slick businessman's haircut with a neat part
on the left side. He was wearing a blue suit under a
long London Fog coat and had a ring on his right
pinkie. I immediately thought of one of those Clint
Eastwood movies when I saw this guy. An inspec-
tor? A detective?

As I approached, the man seemed shaken, possibly afraid that he'd been made. He tried to ease

past me and put on his brimmed hat so that it tipped mysteriously over his brow. As if I couldn't get a good look at him.

"Um . . . excuse me?" I said not five feet away from him. "Is that for Sissy Dickerson?"

"Why . . . uhh . . . yes. It is," he replied.

"Then you're the secret admirer, aren't you?"

He hesitated, lowered his head; there was this defeated expression on his face.

"Well, I—"

"Please, you don't have to answer that. I already know the answer." I stuck out my hand. "How do you do? I'm April, Sissy's best friend. Actually, I'm glad to be meeting you because, really, you've had me curious for the longest time. Won't you join me for a quick drink? Sissy's not home. Won't be for two hours."

"I . . . don't think so."

"Please? I won't keep you long. Promise." Coco Puff was barking now. I couldn't tell if she was hoping for the stranger to say yes as much as I was.

"I'm sorry," the man said. He began to walk away toward the stairway.

"You're a coward, aren't you?" My words seemed to bounce around the hallway walls.

"I beg your pardon?" I swear he flashed me the wickedest stare as he turned back, daring me to repeat myself.

"I said"—I stepped toward him unafraid—"you, mister, are a coward. You drop off your little baskets and notes, scared to face my friend. And now you can't join me for a simple drink? How do you know I can't help you? Make things a little easier for you?" I adjusted the grocery bag in my arms. He was about to say something, but I cut him off.

"But you know what? You go on. I'm sorry I even interrupted your secret delivery." I quickly fit the key in the door as I said this. There was just enough time to slam the door shut behind me. Coward.

Coco Puff hustled toward me, licking at the back of my hand where it supported the groceries. Whew. The moment I put the bag down there was a knock at the door. Coco got to barking again. Dirty Harry, trying to make amends.

"Miss, I apologize. I'm no coward. I just thought . . . listen, I'll stay out here all night if I have to." His voice was muffled a bit by the apartment door between us.

I didn't answer. Let 'im beg.

In a low voice I told Sissy's housepet, "It's okay, girl. Easy now." I stood up again, leaning against the door, waiting for a more earnest plea.

"Please, miss. I actually do need your help. I . . . I'm Sissy's father."

My arms had been folded, but now they fell to my sides. My crooked grin turned to openmouthed shock. My legs almost gave way; I had to grab the doorknob to brace myself. I felt air push out of my lungs as if sucked out by a powerful vacuum.

Sissy's father? I remembered Sissy's exact words. *My mother and father divorced when I was five. I held this against my mother all this time and I haven't seen my father since.*

Like some frightened child, I opened the door some. I trembled and my eyes watered as I peeked through. It didn't matter that the man was white, or that he was claiming to be Sissy's father. This was a moment that touched me personally. Just as Sissy hadn't seen her father in more than twenty years, I hadn't seen my father since birth. So this was my revelation as much as it was hers. "Hold on, would you? I need to put the dog away." In a daze I co-erced Coco Puff to the bedroom and shut her in. When I returned to let Sissy's dad in, he had the basket of cheer in his arms.

"I guess I might as well bring it in," he said as he brushed past me. His cologne struck me hard like some long-lost memory. A wake-up. I had to shake myself from the sudden spell just to close the door. "Where should I put this?" he asked.

"On the table is good. I . . . was just gonna make dinner," I said, trying regain my faculties. "Do you think you'd like to—?"

"No, no, not at all. I think that's way too much too soon, under the circumstances. You know we haven't seen each other in—"

"Twenty years," I intervened.

"Well, yes. To be exact, it has been twenty-one years. So you can imagine how sensitive this is."

"And you figured you'd ease your way back into her life with baskets of cheer?"

He appeared ashamed as he said, "It was all I could think of to start with. But I knew that eventually I'd have to see her face to face. I suppose I was trying to lighten things up."

"Twenty-one years—that's a lot of lightening up," I said as I unpacked the groceries. One raw chicken, honey, tomato sauce, fresh garlic, onions and peppers appeared on the counter, primary ingredients for April's Barbecue Throwdown.

"I don't even know what to call you," I said while I busied myself with food preparation.

"My name is Stuart, but I hope you'll see me as a friend. After all, any best friend of my daughter is a friend of mine."

"Hmm . . . not too bad with the sweet talk, are you?"

"It sort of comes with my profession."

"Oh? What exactly is your profession, Mr. Stuart?" His name felt funny rolling off of my tongue.

"I'm a salesman when it comes down to it. But in real estate we're called brokers."

"I gotcha. So after I hit it big as an author or a national news columnist, I can come to you for help in getting my dream house?"

"Of course. Anything you want. April, did you say your name was? And a writer, huh? Well, if I may say so, April, you certainly are an attractive writer."

"Oh, my, Mr. Stuart—"

"Just Stuart, please."

"Okay," I said, feeling myself blush.

We indulged in a bunch of small talk before I got up the nerve to ask what I really wanted to know. "Tell me, Stuart . . . why has it taken so long for you to come to see your daughter?" Try and sweet-talk your way through that one. "And what makes you think she wants you, or needs you, after all this time?"

"Wow. That's a mouthful," he said. "Here . . . let me help you with the garlic." He came closer to me. "You want the truth, or do you want something that sounds good?"

"You can start with what happened between you and Sissy's mom."

"I'm sure you recognize the difference between Sissy and me," Stuart began.

"Yeah. You're taller, and a little older."

"That's a good one, April. You're a very witty young lady."

"Can we get past the flattery, Stuart?" I realized just then that I had the sharp meat cleaver in my hand. I also had one of the raw chicken thighs pulled aside. "Because this is something that you're eventually going to have to explain to a grown woman who—"

I brought the cleaver down hard, chopping off the thigh and leg.

"—needed you for—"

Now I chopped off the opposite thigh and leg.

"—her entire childhood. For her entire adolescence—"

I bought the sharp blade down again, this time cutting into the center of the bird.

"Her teen years . . . when she lost her virginity!" I had no idea how loud I had been until that blade separated the larger portion of the chicken. It could've been that man's skull on the cutting board as far as I was concerned. I had to fight the pleasure of that idea and put it out of my mind. I was furious, but also devastated.

"April. I'm sorry!" Stuart backed away from me and the meat cleaver.

But his words fell on deaf ears. I was too caught up in the pain and misery of my own life, without a father to protect me, to teach me, to hold me. All my anger and depression was merely suppressed under the facade of religion. I wondered now, more than ever, if my faith and belief in the Lord was merely a replacement for an earthly father. I wondered if my smile was just a mask so that people wouldn't know how I was really feeling. They said April showers bring May flowers. And right now I felt like crying until I drowned.

"Oh dear. April, I'd better go. I can see this is becoming more than I asked for. I'm just a man . . . only human. I can only control some things, not everything. I don't know what you've gone through in your life that has brought you so much sorrow, but if it's any indication of what Sissy will experience, I don't want to be the reason for it." Stuart was putting on his coat, ready to leave. "She doesn't need me to refuel the confusion and anger. I think she'll do just fine without me."

I felt myself slump down onto the kitchen floor.

"April!" He rushed to my aid, his strong hands helping me, lifting me, carrying me to the couch. "Oh God, what have I done?" Moments later I felt a cold, wet cloth dabbing my forehead. "Are you okay, April?"

I heard him, but didn't feel up to responding.

"April, what have I said? Why are you so upset? You must be a hell of a friend to feel Sissy's pain . . . to know what she's gone through."

I pulled at Stuart's sleeve. "You have no idea what it's like to be fatherless. No idea." I took the washcloth from him and wiped my own face. But it didn't stop the tears.

"I'm sorry."

"Stop. Being. Sorry. I don't need your pity." I felt myself growling with conviction. "You're not my father. You're not the solution to my problems. But I know how Sissy feels. My father died a long time ago. I don't even remember seeing his face. But I've been where Sissy's been. Empty-hearted every time the class made Father's Day gifts at school. 'Oh, that's all right. You can make one for your mother,' the teachers said. But it wasn't the same. Every time I saw another kid with their dad, I cried.

It got to a point that I cried every day. For years. So don't even try to understand, because you never will. And if you leave now you'll find some excuse to hide again. Sure, you have that whole woe is me story. Oh, my life took a turn for the worse. Blah, blah, blah. But a woman who's been denied her father ain't trying to hear that, mister. We don't need excuses. We don't need pity. We need our fathers."

He was still, and appeared just as distraught as I felt inside. I felt as though I'd gotten a lot off of my chest, but I knew for sure Sissy had way more to express than me. Shoot. I didn't have a choice. But Sissy's father, regardless what turns his life took, made a decision that separated him from her. Just like me, Sissy was saying, Why did you leave me, Daddy? And, no doubt, this man would have to answer that question somehow, someway, sometime.

I allowed Stuart to hug me, but as much as I needed it, he seemed to need it more. For him, there was twenty-one years of guilt. During our embrace, my heart quickened, and I felt my body shiver. It was a feeling I can't quite explain, despite the fact I make a living describing feelings. This feeling was beyond description. All I know is that it was powerful. And it took total control of my mind.

"I think you'd better leave," I suddenly said.

"Yes. I think so, too," he replied, and he got up from where he knelt by my side. "I'm sorry to have bothered you." He went for his London Fog coat.

I sat up on the couch, stuck for something to

say. "Could you leave your number? Maybe I'll call you . . . see if I can help you out."

After Stuart left, I let Coco Puff out of the bedroom and went back to cooking. Now, thanks to Stuart, along with the barbecue chicken, there'd be champagne and flowers as well. While the chicken was in the oven I went to remove the goodies from the basket. I put the flowers in a vase with water and opened the note that was neatly stuck amongst the variety of fruits.

TO SISSY, FOR NO SPECIAL OCCASION
   BUT THAT
TODAY'S A BEAUTIFUL DAY, AND THAT
   YOU'RE A BEAUTIFUL WOMAN.

The note was signed "Secret Admirer." I chuckled at how Sissy and I had jumped to our own conclusions all this time. We were under the impression that the secret admirer was a love interest—maybe someone from the job, or even in her building. But weren't we the fools? Wow . . . her father. After so many years, who would've guessed?

I stood in the center of Sissy's living room and looked around. Suddenly, I envied her. She had a stable job where her colleagues respected her. She had a secure home and a tough-as-nails way about things. She was attractive, knew what she wanted in life. And now she had her father interested in returning to where he belonged.

I was so happy for her!

No. I wasn't. I was damned jealous. I went into the kitchen, moved the pot of string beans I had smothering on the stove and held the note over the flame so that Stuart's message was reduced to ashes. Afterward, I emptied the basket into the trash and took the bag to the cans at the back of the building. I returned to the apartment and found a mirror to stand in front of.

Good work, April. Jesus wants you to have a daddy. That's why he brought Stuart here today. Now say hi to your daddy. Go ahead.

"Hi, Daddy."

See? Now doesn't that feel good?

# RIVER

**HE TOLD ME** his name was Warren, that he'd never been married and had no children. I acted as if I were more interested in him because of this, that such intimate details were the key to my passion— just to know that he wasn't overburdened and didn't have luggage holding him back from committing to me.

We danced until we were sweaty at Club New York and Warren treated me to an early morning breakfast afterward.

"I don't mean to be nosy," I said. "But how come you ain't got no woman? I mean . . . around where I'm from, the girls would eat you up. The diamond bracelet, the Mercedes with the chrome rims. And you been handin' out money tonight like it's nothin'."

"That's 'cause it is nothin'. I got my hustle goin'

on, ain't got no strings attached to nobody . . .
especially no tricks," Warren replied.

"So you sayin' I'm a trick?" I pretended to be
upset.

"You gotta job?" he asked.

"Not now, but I'm workin' on somethin'."

"And you ain't got no car . . . no assets?"

"No, I don't have no car, baby, but I got plenty
of assets." I added the seductive eyes to my matters
of fact.

"Where?" he asked.

I stood up from our booth in the diner and did a
shameless little turn to show off my body for him.

"Shit, girl, I seen alla that on the dance floor.
Touched it, too—"

"You sure did, baby. And I'm tryin' to get more
of that." I gave Warren that full body massage with
my eyes.

"Whatever. But you need to know that there
ain't nothin' special 'bout you. I can get tits and ass
anywhere . . ."

I was seated again. Discouraged by his words.
And now he was flashing his thick money roll in
my face.

"All I need to do is show you a little of this.
Here—pick that up with your elbows." Warren
dropped a hundred-dollar bill and it floated to the
floor near our booth, embarrassing the shit out of
me. There were only a few people in the diner at
the time, thank God.

"You tryin' to play me?" I asked with a twisted frown.

"Oh . . . not enough? Here's another. And if you wait any longer I'll let the waitress take it."

I knew Warren was on some pimp shit, but I wanted this man somethin' awful. I could taste him in my mouth. "All right, baby. Just for you."

"That's right. The elbows," he emphasized.

I tried to do it quick so that I wouldn't draw attention, but it wasn't as easy as I thought. First, I had to get down on my knees and bend over with my face almost near the floor. Then I had trouble bringing my elbows together on account of my large breasts, not to mention I was getting myself all dirty on the floor. I eventually got the bills wrinkled and then managed to press them between my elbows to lift them to the table. It was the easiest $200 I ever made, but nowhere near the price of the humiliation he put me through. Nevertheless, payback's a bitch. The waitress made a funny face at me when she came with the bill, but I didn't care. I was on a mission.

Back in Warren's Mercedes I asked him what all of that was for, and I asked humbly.

"It was to prove a point to you. See, everybody has a price. Everybody. I don't care who you is. But the point for real was to let you know, like I said, you ain't nothin' but a trick. You ain't got no money comin' in, so you be out tryin' to get with ballers 'nshit. If you see me blingin', you gonna come runnin'. All you bitches is the same."

"Why you gotta say it like that, though?"

"Because I can. And because you need to recognize who's the man."

"I already know who's the man, baby." Boy, are you pushin' your luck!

"Who?" he said through tight lips.

"You the man, Warren."

"Good. So how 'bout you start us off right, before we get to my crib." Warren sat slouched in the driver's seat with one hand on the steerin' wheel. Meanwhile, we were cruisin' down the Major Deegan Expressway at an easy stargazin' pace.

Shit. I didn't wanna do it this way. I had plans to do all this at his place, and I definitely didn't have any plans on him putting his sweaty dick in my mouth. I couldn't even bite it off if I wanted to or else we'd crash. I had to think quick.

"You want me to suck it right now, baby? While you drivin'?" I couldn't believe I was sayin' this shit.

"Don't worry, it ain't shit I'm not used to."

I made this girlish smile at him, before I licked my lips and took a deep breath. Then I scooted over some to run my palm against his chest and down to his zipper. Just before I put my head down in his lap, I noticed that we were approaching the Van Cortlandt Park exit. I was working his limp penis out of its hive until I realized he wasn't circumcised; I also smelled a foul odor. Like spoiled meat. A chill rushed through me, just to think of this nasty worm in my mouth. Pretend, River. Pretend this is your Oscar-winning performance. This isn't what you think. It isn't even what you see. Imagine this is a juicy sausage and that you're at the breakfast table after a ten-mile run. Do it, River . . . he deserves it.

"Baby? I have an idea," I told him after pulling back the foreskin and indulging in a teasing taste test. YECHH! "I wanna make this the best blow job you ever had . . . and, well, I need you to pull over for just a few minutes. I've tried this once before when I was thirteen, and . . . well . . . I got all carsick. And threw up all over my uncle."

"Your uncle?"

I sighed. "Yeah. He used me to make me suck it once a month when he came to New York to visit."

"Aw, shit. I don't want you throwin' up on me, bitch. Hold up."

I smiled a bashful smile as Warren pulled over to the shoulder of the expressway. I peeked up and realized exactly where I was. Cars were zipping by infrequently, too fast to see what we were doing. And it was way too dark, besides.

The mention of "my uncle" did just what I expected: made him real excited. But unfortunately that wouldn't help me with my intentions. I needed him to be limp and soft. Shit.

"Could you ease the seat back some, baby? I'm gonna need some room to get you all-the-way off."

"Shit, you ain't said a thing." Warren said, and the seat gradually eased back.

"Okay, Daddy . . . get ready for the big blastoff. And let me know when you're gonna come. I don't swallow the first time."

"Oh yeah, sure." He wasn't real convincing.

Pretend, River. Pretend. Beef sausage. Delicious beef sausage.

I closed my eyes and took his sour pickle into my mouth.

Meanwhile, I started with the breathing technique I learned a long time ago—how to moan and breathe and suck all at once without choking or taking away from his pleasure. I had to make him feel comfortable and yet excited enough to shoot his load. And yes, I knew he would hold off from telling me he was coming, but it was all part of my act. It was all how you performed that made the blow job work.

I pulled and pushed at Warren's foreskin, his throbbing dick in the embrace of both my hands. I stopped for a short time to ask him if I was doing it like Daddy wants. Men like to be called Daddy, especially while they're inside of one hole or another. Some kinda macho thing.

"Yeah, baby. Just keep on suckin' that mothafucka, keep doin' what you're doin'," he ordered.

"You promise not to come in my mouth?"

"Whatever!" Warren exclaimed, and he pushed my head back down in his lap, my mouth taking him as naturally as an arm in a sleeve.

I moaned.

He sighed.

I whimpered.

Then he yelled and said, "Shit!" He yelled again with pleasure and held my head in place to receive his nasty sperm. I gagged so that it didn't go down my throat and the cream oozed along his twitching muscle.

"Shit, bitch. You got me all messy!"

"If you did like I said I coulda—"

"What'd you say?" Warren was breathing like it was the eighth round of a boxing match, but his voice was threatening. He backslapped me and I fell back against the passenger's seat.

I pretended that this was painful, but in fact I was smiling underneath my hands. I loved this. Absolutely loved it. And now I was breathing heavy, too. I forced myself to make tears and pleaded for mercy. "Please, please, I'm sorry," I exclaimed in my best dying cry. "Please don't beat me, Uncle John."

"Uncle wha—?"

I couldn't see his face, but I could tell he had a strange look about him. "I'll suck it right, Uncle," I said in my best high-school-girl voice.

"Bitch, you outta your fuckin' mind."

I was sure enough that my expression was right before I took my hands away. My vision was wet with tears. The performance was moving along nicely. I went back toward him and caressed his thighs, working up the nerve to follow my plan B. I

lowered my head in his lap and carefully took his
spent dick in hand. All the while, Warren sat there
like a statue. Since he didn't reject my advances, I
went ahead with it. I took an inch of his slimy dick
in my mouth and bit down with every bit of might I
had. I felt my teeth penetrate deep into his organ,
and I swiftly ripped off a chunk as big as a meatball.

Warren jerked back and pushed my head away.
It was a sort of delayed reaction that scared the shit
out of me. Blood squirted out of his open wound in
spurts. Then he hollered, "You bitch!" and buckled
over, grabbing what was left of himself.

I was almost knocked out cold the way my head
hit the passenger side window, but I shook the daze
and reached for Sally down in my purse, on the
floor of the car. It took me two seconds to have her
pointed at Warren. Things were happening so fast
and I was so excited at the success of it all that I
didn't realize the tip of his dick slid down my
throat! I also didn't know I had so much of his
blood on my face.

"What the fuck is wrong with you?!" he cried out.

"Damn, baby . . . you need a doctor," I said. And
then I laughed so hard I could've cried. "Want me
to drive you to the hospital, Daddy?"

"Shit! Shit! Shit! You bit my fuckin' dick off!"

"Listen, lover, this is no time to panic. Now, do I
take you to the hospital or—look here, pay attention
when I speak to you . . ." I used Sally to get Warren's attention, pressing the business end of the .38

Smith & Wesson up to his chin. "Or should I just put you out of your misery right here and now?"

Warren's face was wet with perspiration and he was shaking like a naked man standing in the middle of a snowstorm. His wailing was so loud, he could've been an air raid siren. And I had had just about enough. I looked outside to be sure nobody would see. I leveled the gun at his head.

"This is for the best. Trust me," I said.

Then I squeezed off three shots. The first took off Warren's nose and shattered the driver's side window. The second and third sank into his head, leaving deep, dark, red holes. I quivered, feeling something like a jolt of electricity pushing from my toes, up between my walls and into my breasts, until my nipples hardened. I squeezed my eyes closed to experience the full impact of the moment, a rapture that overwhelmed my senses.

"Wow," I finally said to Warren, as if he were still alive. Then I leaned over and kissed him full on the lips, blood and all. "You were great," I told him. "Now, move over and let this trick drive."

I pulled his body over to the passenger's side and climbed over him so I could drive. His body looked like nothing more than a bag of laundry, lifeless and flopping over on the seat. I directed the car back onto the expressway and kept driving north until an idea came along.

One of my victims had taken me up to his apartment on the far east side of the Bronx. I remembered him—Patrick—parking at an all-night car wash across the street. It was one of those self-service places where you put a couple dollars in quarters into a machine, and sat in your car and let 'er rip.

I drove off of the expressway just before reaching Yonkers and headed east to where I remembered Patrick lived. Poor Patrick. Why all these men try to be macks and pimps, I'll never know. I swear that shit only helps me. It motivates me to fulfill my goal: kill the mothafuckas. And as I pulled into the car wash I couldn't help amusing myself, wondering if he was still slumped there, across the street in that apartment, with that big kitchen knife stuck in his head.

It was nearing midnight when I lowered the window to feed quarters into the machine. I didn't bother raising the window, either. I just let the water and soap come into the car, getting me, Warren and everything else all wet. Eventually, I directed the car over to where the vacuums were stationed and left it sitting there.

I walked wet and uncomfortable for blocks until I found the #4 train station at Jerome Avenue. By the time a train came, I was partially dry, enough to have a seat and look as normal as some of the other night crawlers who boarded. I paid a homeless man two bucks for his baseball hat to cover my messy hair. I didn't care that it was dirty or that it had been through God knows what, I just needed to somehow cover up and stay inconspicuous. At least until I got home, where Brandon was waiting to pleasure me.

"RIVER? HI. THIS is Victor. I hope you're not avoiding me. I mean, this is your number, isn't it? So far, I've called you like six times and I haven't spoken to you once. I got your message the other day, but I think I told you I'm not home during evenings which is when you called . . . Anyway, I'm not blaming you, I just want us to get together. Get to know each other better. Call me, huh?"

The message was cut short after Victor's plea. I smiled at how I was handling him: teasing him enough to make him want more, and yet not giving him any more details than he needed to have. I figured now was the time to finish him.

I wasn't the least bit tired after my night out with Warren. Sure, we danced and ate, and, yes, I bit off the tip of his dick and shot him to shit, but I was so full of energy. I was ready to run a marathon! "Sorry, Brandon. No coochie tonight. I got another job to do. And God knows how I been waiting for this one," I explained things to my dog as I fed him.

Then I returned Victor's phone call. Of course I used my second unregistered cell phone so that there'd be no record; no relationship between my call and our late-night meeting. "Victor? Victor, pick up. It's me, River."

I heard a loud squealing noise, the feedback

between the answering machine and the telephone receiver.

"River? River! Damn, baby, I thought you were—whoa . . . one o'clock in the morning? This must be the call I've been waiting for."

"A booty call? Is that what you mean, Victor?"

"I was just kidding, River. But now that you mention it . . . *is* this a booty call?"

I laughed to lighten up the mood. No, jackass, it's a murder call. I forced a sensual tone to ask him, "Would you like it to be a booty call?"

Victor stammered, "I, uh, y-yeah. Why not?"

Hmmph. You was a mack daddy the other day with your I-know-you-want-me attitude. Have you gone soft? "Give me your address again. I'll be there within the hour."

After we hung up, I went to make myself smell so fresh and so clean. I put on a delicious outfit: the pale rose velour pullover and matching leggings would do. Under it I wore a set of matching underwear, black silk bra and panties. Blue suede hiking boots completed the look. I wanted it to be obvious that I'd come to fuck and get fucked. For a finishing touch I put on a soft and bouncy light brown wig with hair that fell to my shoulders. There was no time to fix up what the car wash did to my own hair.

Just like that—and a couple of perfume mists—and I was out the door once again. This time, I had my big Samsonite suitcase in tow. I loaded it in the secondhand Nissan Sentra I borrowed from the neighbor, and headed to Pelham Parkway, an area I knew to be a quiet, residential community on the far west end of the Bronx. I left the suitcase in the car and strolled toward the doorway of Victor's home as casually as I knew how. I knew, however, that he'd be watching me, wondering: why is this woman coming to give herself to me so suddenly?

You'll soon find out, damn fool.

To take my mind off of the full extent of my circumstances, I pretended to be interested in the neighborhood, and I looked worriedly to the left and right. The houses were very close here, a small problem that thank God I was prepared for.

Victor was waiting there inside the doorway. After all, it was pitch-black out in front of the house, with only the streetlights, walkway and stoop. I might've gotten mugged or something.

"Well, well . . . no problem finding me, huh?"

"Nope. You know what they say about a person who wants something bad enough."

"No, what do they say, River?" We were in a soft embrace as he said this. And I craned my head back some to answer.

"Well, silly, if you want something bad enough, you usually find a way to get it." And I planted a kiss on Victor's lips; one that he'd never forget, as if we'd been friends forever, and lovers on occasion. "You okay?" I asked him with my arms draped around his neck.

"Oh—yeah. Fine. Just fine."

"Well then, let's have some fun," I said, and stepped ahead of him.

I found Victor's home to be small, and lacking a woman's touch. There was evidence of a fast food dinner on the table. Dishes were stacked in his kitchen sink. And in the bedroom I noticed some dirty clothes peeking out from under the bed, as if he'd stashed them there before I came. I ignored the quick fixes and got down to business.

"Mind if I make myself comfortable?" I asked, but hardly waited for an answer. I needed to be fucked. And I needed it now.

"Wow," Victor said, gaping. "You were serious about this, weren't you?" I already had my top off and was now wiggling out of my pants.

"Unclasp my bra, lover." I turned my back to Victor and measured my surroundings as I did. His wallpaper had at least a hundred different shades of brown that seemed to rain down in tickertape strips. I swear, the shit was makin' me dizzy just lookin' at it. Of course the linen on the bed didn't match, some kind of olive green fabric. The carpet was a dull red. There was an old wooden night table with the book *What a Woman Wants* lying on its lower shelf, so I guessed he didn't expect me to see it. A folded newspaper was lying on top of the table along with a clock radio with bright digital numbers reading 1:30 A.M. Some kind of skinny lamp, a beeper and a set of keys also accessorized the tabletop.

As soon as I got out of my bra and panties, I went to close Victor's blinds as well as the ugly brown curtains. Finally, I crawled onto his king-size bed. At least that was correct; big enough to handle the "fun" I had in store.

"What're you waitin' for?" I asked. The question seemed to shake him out of his stupor.

"Uh . . . oh . . . damn, River. I can't wait to get my hands on you."

"Then hurry up, before my horse and buggy turns into a pumpkin and I change my mind." I lay there and watched him fumble with his buttons, then his zipper; then he almost fell trying to get his pants off.

I laughed so loud he took offense at it. "Don't get an attitude, mister. You look like a clown," I dared to say.

"A clown, huh?" Victor was in his boxers now and about to get on the bed. "I'll show you a clown, you—"

"Hey! Watch yo' mouth, nigga. Don't get me mixed up with that ho you had here yesterday. If you talk dirty, there betta be a reason."

"Huh? What—?"

"Don't play me, nigga. Just make sure you twist me as good as you did her." I ignored Victor's surprised look and got on my hands and knees. My face was flat against his pillows. "Come hit it," I said with closed eyes and a deep breath. Then I felt his hands on my body, his lips kissing my ass, the backs of my thighs, and the soles of my feet. The whole thing had me shaking with joy: he was doing this exactly as I'd detailed for him on our date just a week and a half earlier.

"I LIKED YOU the minute I laid eyes on you, River. I hope we'll be able to get to know each other better." Victor had put on the whole Romeo act for me over dinner. He talked soft, performed the usual courtesies and made himself seem like the ultimate man. But I knew better. I knew it was all an act; that shit most men do in the beginning of a relationship. And it lasts all the way up to the bedroom. Once they get the pussy, shit changes. Macho man!

"Oh, yeah? So soon? I mean, we just met. How can you tell?" I had been putting on the act, eating my food all proper—not licking the flavor off of my fingers or lips, using a napkin like a nice girl with home training.

"I just . . . I can tell. It's a vibe I get."

"A vibe, huh? You mean, something like our women's intuition?"

"I guess."

"Well, what if I told you I'm a freak behind closed doors? Would you still like me? Would you still want to get to know me better?"

"I . . . uh . . . what is this, a trick question?"

"And I'm waiting for a trick answer," I told him.

"Well . . . I guess I'd need to know more about you—I mean, that's the whole point here, isn't it? Dinner? Conversation? The movie?"

"Yeah, but let's keep it real, Victor. Every man wants a good freak in the bedroom, don't they? Unless you're . . . funny."

Victor laughed loudly. A few neighboring diners were looking in our direction. I didn't care. Victor took my hand across the table. "River, I can guarantee you—I am not funny."

"Okay, so let's get past the bullshit. You're attracted to me, I'm attracted to you . . . are we on the same page?"

Victor worked up a nod to mean yes.

"And you're a grown-ass man and I'm a grown-ass woman, right?" I took my hand back and wiped the back of my wrist against my lips.

"Y-yeah."

"Then, good. We're done here tonight. I'm not really hungry to start with . . ." I pushed my plate aside, most of the chicken was uneaten. Then I said, "I have something to do." And boy did I ever. I had a date with a pimp named Roger. (He swore he could make me a good ho after just one night together. Of course I accepted the challenge.)

"But what I want you to do is give me a call tomorrow. Sleep on it. Imagine you and me together, in bed for the first time . . . me on my hands and knees. I mean, we've hardly kissed but I'll have all my shit wide open for you . . . on your bed . . ."

AND SURE ENOUGH, after days and days of making Victor wait, here we are in his bed, with me on my hands and knees, my ass up in the air, my face and my soft cries buried in his pillow. I was really into this too, breathing so heavily that the aroma of hair grease in his pillow was filling my lungs.

"Mmm . . ." I moaned when Victor continued following those instructions from last week. He was painting my calves now, using his tongue and saliva and working his way toward my love factory. Eventually he reached my wet hood and lapped at it like I told him. "That's a boy. That's my Brandon," I said in soft cries. Victor stopped for half a second, probably to protest about me calling him Brandon but I reached back and pulled his face back into my stuff.

"Don't blow my high, baby. I'm trying to picture you as my dog . . . Oh baby, lick that coochie. Yeah."

Obediently, Victor ran his tongue up and down the crack of my ass and in and out of my holes until I screamed for mercy. I couldn't hold my own desires in any longer. I needed to have him inside of me. He was hung like a goddamn monster.

Before I invited him in, I got on my back and had him kneel over my face. I took his dick in my mouth and reached up to claw at his chest with my fingernails. I felt him shake and quiver, and his dick was growing harder in my mouth. I kept my eyes open. The whole time, watching Victor squirm like this was painful. His face twisted into a bunch of angry, strange, erratic expressions.

One of those expressions reminded me of Warren. Only then did I remember that I'd had another man's dick in my mouth just hours earlier. The thought got me that much more excited. I grabbed Victor's rock-hard muscle and massaged it with both hands, building up my jerking motions at every chance. There was a point when all my conscious actions turned unconscious, and I lost control.

With his groans and my muffled sighs filling the room, driving the excitement, I allowed Victor to ejaculate down my throat in a constant stream. I couldn't taste it because it was past my taste buds in swallows. And I make it a rule not to swallow, especially since I didn't know shit about these guys I was killing. I mean, I didn't want to catch AIDS or anything.

But there were those few who were exceptions. Roger was an exception. I knew I was gonna serve him a vicious death, so I figured it was only right. There was one other guy, Ed I believe it was, who I drove a car into. Crushed him between the front fender and a brick wall. And now, here was Victor. I had something real nice in store for him. No doubt about it.

"Where you goin,' baby?"

"Bathroom," Victor said. "To wash up. We're done, aren't we?"

"Not even close! Nigga, I'm tryin' to eat your ass out. Can't I get my rocks off?"

Victor sucked his teeth and said, "In a minute. Damn, bitch. You is a freak." And he slipped into the bathroom.

*Just like I thought. The mothafucka's already changin' his tune. Now I'm a bitch, huh?* I was a little exhausted now, but I had enough energy to carry this out. I pulled out a cigarette, lit it and lay back on Victor's bed. No ashtray, I just flicked the ashes anywhere. *Shit. What's a dead man gonna do? Argue about my cigarette ashes? I don't think so.* I even finished the smoke before Victor came back out.

"Damn, nigga? What'd you do? Monthly hygiene?"

"I—what's that smell? Was you smokin' up in here?"

"Yeah. It's all right with you, isn't it?"

Victor sucked his teeth and said, "Fuck no, it isn't all right with me. How you gonna come in a mothafucka's house and just blow that nasty shit all in my bedroom? Fuckin' ho!"

I pretended to be ashamed, hoping to ease the man's anger. "I'm sorry, sugar. Come and let me make it up to you," I pleaded. Again he sucked his teeth and approached the bed. I thought the anger had gone until he noticed the ashes on the bed.

"Shit, bitch!" he shouted, then he slapped me hard across the face. It spun me back onto the bed. "You put your mothafuckin' ashes on my bed?!"

"Oh God! No, Victor! Please! Please don't beat me." I was secretly getting off on this.

"Beat you? I'ma whip you until the cops come knockin'."

I didn't get a word in before I felt something whip my naked ass. I screamed when the pain shot through me. It stung, but I got some kind of weird thrill from it.

"Wait! Wait! Victor, please!" I rolled away from him. Out of reach of his leather belt. "Let's be adult about this—" I began desperately.

"Adult?" Victor climbed onto the bed and was quickly back at me with the belt. He whipped my leg. I scrambled to get away. He got to me again, the belt catching my back. I cried out.

"Victor, listen to me!" I had my hands up to him and he actually took a break and listened.

"You wanna whip me with that belt, okay. But let's do it another way. We don't need neighbors or cops in this." Victor made a strange face in response to my comment. "Yes . . . I said it's okay. I'll let you whip me. I deserve it since I was wrong for droppin' ashes on your bed. But don't kill me."

I approached Victor and hesitantly took his hand. I led him to the edge of the bed and I got on the floor, the upper half of my body flat on the bed. I pulled his pillows close so I could bury my head.

"Okay, Uncle . . . punish me." I saw Victor's face before I again pressed my face into the greasy pillows. There was a pause, but I soon felt the belt whipping my ass like I was an animal. The pillows absorbed all my screams and tears as Victor hit me again and again. I felt my nipples harden enough to break off. I squeezed my pussy between every strike of the leather belt, bracing myself for the spasms that came with each whipping.

All the while, Victor was rambling: "Bitch! I'ma wear yo' ass out! You ain't nothin' but a goddamn whore! You and yo' momma! Who's your uncle?!"

"You are."

"Louder!" And with each statement he belted me good 'n hard. When he was finished, my ass and the backs of my thighs were throbbing just like old times. I could also feel my own juices oozing down the inside of my legs. I must've climaxed four or five times.

"When you feel up to it get your shit and get the fuck out," Victor said. Through my tear-blurred vision, I could see him take a leak in the bathroom, then he came back to the bed and attempted to sleep, leaving me to take care of myself.

I murmured, "I love you, Uncle, I love you so much . . ." I repeated it until I felt my eyes close. I rested there on the floor for what seemed like days, but it was actually hours. It was Victor's loud snoring that woke me. The digital clock radio read

4:19. I didn't have much time, so I got myself up, paying no mind to the pain about my lower body, and got dressed. I went outside to the Nissan, and pulled the Samsonite from the trunk. Tools of the trade.

Back in Victor's bedroom, I eased onto the bed and stretched him out into a spread-eagle position. He slept like a goddamn bear. Regardless, if it hadn't gone down this way, I would've tricked him into it anyhow. What he didn't know wouldn't hurt him.

Ha.

I attached leather restraints to his wrists first and tied them to the front legs of the bed. Then the ankles. The straps were extra-long, so they easily reached across the king-size bed. Then I lit a cigarette.

"Okay, playboy. Wake that ass up."

Victor was still snoring, even after I blew Newport smoke in his face. So I took one big drag to blaze the tip to a sizzling orange, then pressed the cigarette into his testicles.

"AAAAHHHHH!!!" he screamed. "Fuck, fuck, fuck!"

His shout reminded me of that couple in Hartsdale; that producer Barry saying, "Fuck!" when his wife surprised us. I had to laugh to recall that bit. But back to Victor . . .

"Hmmm . . . a little tied up at the moment, are you?" I was humored at how Victor was so surprised to be in restraints. But then, out of nowhere, he started pissing on himself. I covered my mouth, actually amazed at the sight of his limp dick doin' its own thing.

"River! Take these fucking straps off of me."

"No, I'm afraid not, baby. Oh my . . . he won't stop pissing. Tell 'im to stop before you get all messy."

"River! Get these fucking straps off!"

"A little demanding , huh? Tell you what. Before I cut you to pieces, I'll suck it one more time to make it all better. Would you like that?"

Victor's reply was unrecognizable; something of a maddened growl.

"Now, we can't have all this noise, soo . . ." I took a roll of gray duct tape from the various items I'd laid on the bed, ripped some off and went to put it over Victor's mouth.

"I need you to keep the peace." Victor tried to wiggle his head away, but I managed to zip his lips.

"See? Now that's not so bad. Now let me try and make my little baby nice and comfortable." I didn't have too much more time to fool around if I expected to be out of his house by 5 A.M., when early workers might leave their homes. I didn't want to be seen by anyone. So I toyed with his dick some, just to get last licks, because after this morning, nobody would ever be pleasured by this monster again. Ever. "Okay. Time to go to work."

I put on my goggles and gloves. I bent down to

open the Samsonite on the floor. I took out the buzz saw and placed it on the bed. Victor squirmed and carried on like a wild man in restraints, but his efforts were a waste of time. I tightened the straps and turned on the television. Tom and Jerry reruns. You gotta love 'em.

I plugged in the extension cord and started up the buzz saw.

Victor was going crazy now, and the sight of him made me think of a scene in *Scarface*. I realize that things like this had been done before, and maybe that's where I got this mad idea in the first place. Oh well, I guess everything has been done before by somebody, somewhere.

"This is going to hurt me more than it will you . . . it's rare that you run into a dick like yours . . ." I took a deep breath. "Oh well. Shit happens. Hang on for the experience of a lifetime."

I started with his dick. They didn't do that in *Scarface*. The saw cut right through that thing like a cheap pork sausage. Blood began squirting, just like when he was pissing minutes earlier. "Good, good. Now for the leg. Hang on, baby!" I growled.

Victor's cries were muffled by the duct tape, but I could sense his pain.

"It's all right, hon . . . just think of me as the saw hits the bone." The saw chewed into the skin, flesh and bone like the parting of the Red Sea. I had to apply some pressure as I sank deeper into the bones and tendons, but the job was moving along nicely. Messy, but worth the fuss. Blood sprayed everywhere, especially on my clothes, face and hair. I didn't care. The smell of blood . . . the sight of blood . . . the taste of blood . . . it just got me all wet between my sugar walls.

Finally, the first leg was severed all the way and I took a quick break. I don't know what Victor was thinking, shaking like he was . . . his eyes all bugged out as though they were about to pop out of his head. I wondered if he was enjoying this as much as I was.

"You all right, baby?" Victor didn't answer. He just lay there, still as stone. Then his eyes began to close and the shaking slowed until it stopped altogether. I blew him a kiss and wiped my goggles.

"Well . . . let me know when I've finished. I'm sure you will appreciate my work. Hold on, boo!" Again I started the motor and went for his opposite leg, right where his thigh connected with his groin. Wow. I thought I'd drown in all that blood. It was soaking into my leggings, deepening their rose color to a dark red. I wished I'd brought a raincoat but it was too late for that. There'd be a next time when I'd come more prepared.

I hadn't counted on Victor being in a coma, or dead, but he was definitely one or the other. I wanted him to be conscious for my whole project. Dick, legs, and arms. But it looked like he only lasted to see my work on the first leg. Oh well.

I finished the job for the hell of it. Then I dragged

all four body parts along his ugly carpet until the blood created a giant heart. I also dipped my hands in the pool of blood on the bed and made a bunch of hearts on his walls. I figured the place needed a woman's touch; some large and small hearts couldn't hurt. I tossed the limbs back on the bed, laughing at how backward it all looked, then I took the Polaroid camera out of the Samsonite and snapped a dozen photos. I left one beside Victor's face, and did a semi-cleanup. I went to run water over the electric saw and extension cord. I had a fresh change of clothes in the suitcase, so I'd have something bloodless to wear after a nice hot shower.

Everything was smooth until the knock at the front door.

Careful to keep my face hidden, I peeked out the front window to find a man standing on the front landing with his hands on his hips like he had a big attitude. I couldn't imagine who the hell this was. I was just glad that it wasn't the police. Maybe an angry neighbor coming to gripe about the noise from the saw?

I couldn't afford to have this guy calling the police, so I grabbed Sally from my purse and went to answer the door without opening it. "Who is it?"

"Whaddya mean, who is it? Who are you?"

"Never mind. What can I do for you? It's not a good time, we're tryin' to get some sleep."

There was no response, but I could've sworn I heard the guy curse. Maybe he was leaving.

I went back to the window and found the man looking here and there, in the mailbox, under a potted plant. I wondered what the hell he was looking for, but before I could guess I heard a key being fitted into the lock. Oh shit! He has a key? I knew now that this was more than a neighbor. How much more, I didn't know. And I didn't care either. I stood ready with Sally.

# SISSY

SO I HAD to come right out and ask April if this was some kind of lesbian thing. Her wanting to move in.

"I mean, no offense. I'm just not down with it. I like dick, April. Strickly dickly. I just haven't found the right package to go with it," I told her.

"Nothing like that, Sissy. I'm a woman of God. How could you ask such a thing?"

"Well, I've never seen you with a man, April."

"And you never asked."

"Okay. So come clean. Call this my official policewoman's interrogation. Who is he? Where's he work, where's he live and if you were to move in, would he be moving in, too?" I hoped I wasn't coming on too strong, but I was curious. And I was especially serious about her having some strange man up in my apartment. All I'd need in my life is to respond to a domestic dispute at my own place.

And I wouldn't hesitate to bust a cap up in some guy for hurtin' April. That's my girl.

"Sissy, I'm not even seeing anyone right now. I have my eye on somebody, but it's nothing serious. Not yet, anyway."

"Not yet, huh?"

"Well . . . it has to be right by God, Sissy. I'll do a whole lot of praying on it. And you know I'm not gonna be with him until marriage. No more of that fornicating. When you're born again, you've gotta do everything by the Good Book. Has to be right by the Lord."

Oh brother. Can this girl be any more wholesome?

"April, how about giving me a little something about the guy? Is he from the Bronx?"

"I think."

"Does he at least have a job?"

"I'm sure of it. But I haven't gotten the juicy on him yet. You know if I knew I'd tell you, girl."

"I should hope so." I wondered if she was hiding something.

"But about the apartment . . . I don't plan on any visitors whatsoever. I'm not trying to butt in your private world. I just thought it would be convenient . . . that I'd be safe, and you, too. I mean, there's some kind of serial killer out here, right?"

"But she's killing men," I said.

"She?" April lit up like the sun. "It's a woman?"

Oh shit. That was inside stuff. I took a deep breath. "April, you didn't hear that from me." Damn.

"You said she. Oh, come on, Sissy! This is like the biggest story of the century! Why wouldn't you share that with me? It's not like I would reveal my sources."

I thought about it. I never brought the job home with me. Never talked about police work except with Maritza, or at police headquarters.

"Please, Sissy? You can count on me to keep things confidential. That's my word."

"And you moving in and all, if I ever heard about you exposing me, I'd beat your ass . . ."

"Oh Sissy! You mean you'll do it?! You'll have me as a roommate?"

"Housemate. Don't twist things up, people might jump to conclusions. Housemate."

April was so happy she jumped up and charged me with a big hug. "Thank you, thank you, thank you. You won't be sorry, Sissy. That's a promise. I'll never get in your hair. I'll be as quiet as a mouse. I'll do my share of the chores . . . feed Coco Puff."

"Easy, April. We're not getting married here." April's hug felt funny, with her breasts pressed up against mine and all. I caught a chill, but I quickly shook it off.

"So . . . you'll give me the juicy-juice on the Pink Heart murders?"

"You got a pen and pad?" April couldn't be happier. She picked through her handbag and produced the tools of her trade. Where I had my Glock 9 and handcuffs, April had her pen and pad.

"Okay, shoot. You said this was a woman's work."

"It is a woman's work. FBI experts are finding strands of hair from different wigs. One guy was left dead in the lot of a car wash up in Riverdale, with the head of his penis bitten off. All, or most, of these men were involved with various women or cheating on their wives or common-law wives."

"Excuse me for being objective, Sissy, but how do you know these men weren't gay? I mean, the hair could be from those ponytails you add to your own hair. So what if it's a transvestite, or a cross-dresser? I mean, that bit about the penis being bit off—"

"I agree with you to an extent. Sure, a man could've done that. The other day a guy over near Pelham Parkway was cut to shreds, and apparently his lover walked in on the event. Then he got done, too. But realistically, April, this was the work of a woman.

"A few of these victims were men Maritza and I met on disturbance calls. I mean, these were definitely no homosexuals. One husband on White Plains Road worked in the city sewers all day. At night, he came home and took out his frustrations on his wife. Another guy lived with his girlfriend in Co-op City. Apparently he was selling drugs out of the apartment, and he left his girl to watch things for an hour or two and she got robbed. We responded to a call about a domestic dispute, but come to find out the reason that the boyfriend beat his girl's ass was because she 'allowed' the robbery to happen. I mean, this guy actually expected his girlfriend to say no when the thugs ordered her to open the house safe."

"So, the boyfriend beat her for that?"

"Two black eyes, a broken nose and cigarette burns on her breasts."

"Wow."

"And she wouldn't press charges, April. They never do. They always come up with some god-damn excuse. 'I fell!' Or 'We were having wild sex!' You name it, I've heard it."

"Did you ever think of this serial killer as some kind of Death Wish chick? A black widow, or even an avenger of some kind?"

"You bet I did. In fact, I smile every time I hear about the victim's background. It's always the same: womanizer . . . pimp . . . adulterer. These men are no good, April. She's on some kind of mission. You want to know the crazy thing? And April, if you repeat this to anybody . . . I own a gun, you know?" I growled playfully at my friend.

"Tell me, Sissy."

"It's a good thing I'm a cop, because I kinda like her profession. I'd even help her."

"Don't say that, Sissy. You're no killer. You can't even stand the sight of blood. Remember the car accident in Brooklyn? The stabbing around our way? You're a pussycat."

"What're you tryin' to say, heifer? That I can't do my job?"

April sucked her teeth. "No, chile. I'm just saying that you're a nice person. Too nice to kill anyone."

"But if I had to, I would."

"I guess it goes with the job. Let's just pray you never get into that situation."

"Pray hard," I said, knowing how cruel the streets were.

"Okay. So let's assume this is a woman," April continued. "Do you guys have any leads? Are you at least coming close to catching her?"

"Honestly? I don't work homicide. This is their problem. I can tell you they're turning up the volume since the Pelham Parkway killings. That man was literally cut to shreds, April. The woman used a damned electric saw and took off his arms and legs. She even cut off his penis. They think she flushed it down the toilet because it was nowhere to be found—plus they found traces of blood in the bathroom."

April shivered, and her pen stopped moving.

"Am I being too graphic for you? I mean—"

"No, no; not at all. Just the idea of it—I never heard of anything like this. A bit gory."

"What, you been living with your head in the sand, April? This is New York, girl. Mob hits, triple homicides and gang murders. You name it, New York has seen it. I'm sure there are some horrors out there that we haven't even heard of yet . . .

bodies at the bottom of the Hudson and whatnot. But for real, it's nothin' but evil streets out here, April. Anything goes."

"I suppose. But I've been focusing on brighter colors, Sissy." April went on to explain how we only see the colors we focus on. "It's only now that I'm opening up to so much violence."

"And why is that?"

"Money. It seems like that's where all the stories are. That's all publishers are looking for. And I won't pay my bills without work."

"So you figured I could help you with all the inside—what'd you call it?—the juicy-juice on crime and violence . . ." April had some guilt in her expression. "Hey, listen, it's not a problem with me. Do you, baby. I can't be mad. I hope you go on to do big things. Then I could say I knew you way back when."

"Thanks, Sissy. I appreciate your understanding."

"Not a problem."

APRIL MOVING IN was somewhat of a relief, I must say. She contributed so much with the cooking (she makes a mean barbecue chicken dinner), the cleaning and even helped to take care of Coco Puff. She had a lot of questions about the job, but I didn't mind. The fact is, telling her so much helps to take a lot of pressure off my shoulders; something like therapy. I feel like I'm unloading things. More important, she was absolutely right about us

being safer as a team, instead of being single
women living in our own separate apartments. Our
own worlds. And indeed, there was a killer on the
loose. Surely more than just one.

Maritza was beginning to take the homicides personally, especially since the two killings on Pelham
Parkway. I didn't voice any opinion, but the two
dead men were Puerto Rican, like Maritza. And not
for nothin', but she didn't give the Pink Heart murders such focus or consideration until her people
started gettin' whacked. That's that association by
assimilation shit. Like, her Puerto Rican pride is
spillin' over into her job.

Shit, I don't like to get racial when it comes to
the job, and I didn't think twice about the serial
killer finishing off a bunch of no-good negroes. All
I knew was that men were being killed. Human be-
ings. I didn't divide them into sections like a box
of chocolates. With all the different thoughts clut-
tered in the closet on my shoulders, color-coding
crime wasn't one of them.

"Well, you haven't said too much about the
killings, Sissy. And we usually talk about everything," said Maritza.

"True enough. Maybe it's because that stuff is
out of our league. Homicide and the FBI have
enough masterminds dealing with that stuff to
cover me, you and the other hundred thousand
heads of NYPD. Why should I waste my energy?"

"You don't feel a little threatened? I mean, a few

of those murders were kinda close to home . . . men we actually dealt with on domestic calls . . ."

I didn't answer, just shrugged.

"And if not that, how about the locations of all these killings? Webster. Randall. Washington. Harding. White Plains Road. Jesus, Joseph and Mary, Sissy, this is our home. I have family here . . ."

"I understand, Maritza. But honestly, all we can really do is keep our own homes safe. We can't protect everybody."

"Well, aren't you the smug one with a wild killer on the loose?" Martiza snapped.

"Not smug, really. Just following the standard. What was it that you drilled into my head when I first started as your partner? Don't take this shit personal; if you do, it could get you killed. Didn't you say that? Now here we are almost two years later and you're trippin'!"

"You still don't gotta be all smug about it," she grumbled.

I chuckled at that and suggested, "How about the drive-through, my treat?"

"I'm watching my weight," she replied. "Gotta lay off them doughnuts." And them pink hearts.

"Well, at least have a cup of tea or coffee with me. It's almost time for a break."

"A break, huh. The last time we were about to take a break, someone had to be rushed to Montefiore for the stab wounds."

"Her man's still at large, ain't he?"

"Yup. I hope we catch him first, too. He might not make it to headquarters." Maritza was always acting tough. And I always had no comment. But I know she'd always remember who the real Super-woman was. Seniority or no seniority.

We pulled up to the window of Dunkin' Donuts at Boston Post Road and Conner Street. I ordered a blueberry muffin and a coffee, light and sweet. Maritza ordered the tea.

"You can eat anything and still be a tight body, Sissy. I wish I was dealt your cards."

"Wanna switch places? Wear my shoes for a day? I bet you'll want that petite body of yours back before you can say Bally's Total Fitness."

"Is that how you keep in shape?" Maritza asked as the aproned attendant went to get our order. "Health club membership?"

"Actually, besides going to Bally's three times a week, I have tae kwon do classes, and I also run between two and three miles every morning."

"Whoa. Now that's a little bit too much for me. Your plate must be full. No wonder you don't have time for a man."

"One day. That is, if the Pink Heart Lady don't kill 'em all first."

"See! She is on your mind! You do agree it's a she." I threw my hands up playfully. "Okay. You caught me red-handed. Yes, I agree that it's a she; yes, she is on my mind. But no, I'm not concerned about her . . . not to the point I'm losing sleep. Actually, if you wanna know the truth, I had a dream about catching her the other night."

"Oh my . . ." Maritza said to me, before she turned to the girl at the window. "Thanks, dear. How much?"

"It's all right. On the house," answered the girl.

That's when I spoke up. "Oh no, baby—that's not how it's supposed to go down."

"But my boss says—"

"It doesn't matter what your boss says. You can't go giving police breaks all the time, it leads to other things. Then before you know it, you'll be on your knees in a perverted cop's squad car, and all because of some free doughnuts and coffee. How much for the food, baby?" I was determined to pay.

"Uh . . . oh . . ." The poor girl looked confused. She didn't know what to say. On one hand, her boss had told her to give out free food, and on the other, I was directing her to take my money.

"Here, Maritza. Give it to her." I stuffed a few dollars in my partner's hand and urged her to pass it on. When we left, I was about to get into this whole explanation of police ethics with Maritza, except a call came in.

"Respond to a domestic dispute at 1725 Gun Hill Road . . . See a woman only identified as Nancy about an assault claim, over." The dispatcher was almost always a woman.

"That's a ten-four," I said while Maritza maneuvered the squad car into a U-turn and shot up Boston Post Road.

"Gun Hill? Do we know that address?"

"Gun Hill, yes; 1725, no. Sounds like a new situation."

Lights flashing and siren screaming, we raced up Boston Post Road.

Four minutes later, we were surprised to find out that 1725 wasn't a residence after all. It was a used-car lot sandwiched between a real estate broker's office and a White Castle restaurant. And sure as the sun was going down, there was a crowd gathered in the center of the lot with a man and woman going at it like prized fighting roosters.

Of course Maritza propelled the squad car onto the lot, nearly bulldozing the bystanders. This was just one of the many ways that officers imposed themselves, using their vehicles as a show of power. You get used to it after a while. It's more or less routine. Maritza and I jumped out of the car and went into action, nightsticks in hand.

"Clear the way," Maritza ordered.

"Break it up. Let's go. Find someplace else to stand," I barked. And the small crowd quickly disbursed. What I saw as folks backed up was shocking.

A black man standing about six feet tall was standing over a woman almost half his size and weight. She was on the gravel of the lot with most of her hair in his tight grip. Apparently, by the woman's appearance—clothes tattered and her face scratched—she had been dragged and beaten. I wondered just how much of this those bystanders had watched.

"Let that woman go, right now," Maritza commanded. I wasn't much for words at this point. I went right up and grabbed the big man's arm and cuffed his wrist. He still hadn't let go of the woman's hair so I had to use force. I struck the backs of his knees with my nightstick and he instantly buckled. Now he was the one on the ground with Maritza's foot on his neck. I twisted his opposite arm back until both wrists were cuffed.

"Now you be cooperative, big boy, or else things will get worse from here." Maritza, the bully.

I helped the woman to her feet and escorted her to the squad car where she'd be comfortable on the backseat. She looked so worn and so abused that it was hard to begin my procedure. Hard to be insensitive to her circumstances, or overlook the injuries to her face.

"Can you tell me your name?" I asked, compassionate, at least.

She was sobbing now, but she managed to get a few words out.

"N-Nancy. Nancy Grimes," she said through swollen lips.

"And who's that man who beat you?"

"He ain't . . . he ain't beat me. It's my fault. I was in the wrong.

Freddie caught me with my boss . . . Mista Brown."

"Freddie? That's his name? Is that your husband? Boyfriend?"

The woman was already making excuses for the guy. I just needed the facts for now, but I could already sense the bottom line.

"That's my man and baby-father."

"Right, right. And who's Mr. Brown?"

"He my boss. He back in the office."

"How old are you, Nancy?"

"Twenty-three."

"And you work here? What's your job?"

"Mista Brown's assistant. But Freddie said I can't work here no more."

"Where do you live, Nancy?"

"Round the corner, on Laconia. Round near the back of the bowling alley."

As I questioned Nancy, I could see Maritza escorting Freddie to a minivan where she had him bend over on the hood, frisking him for weapons and whatnot. Nancy also looked toward Maritza and Freddie, and now she carried on with the screaming.

"No! Nooo! Don't lock him up! He ain't do nothin'!" The woman's screams were like the call of the wild, turning the volume way up on an already unpredictable atmosphere. And before I could catch her, she was up and out of the car. She slipped past me and ran towards my partner and her "baby-father."

"Shit! Garcia!" I shouted at the top of my lungs but this broken bitch was hauling her wild-ass hips toward Maritza, closing the gap between the squad car and the minivan in record time. I got after her, but not before she leaped onto Maritza in a reckless attempt to stop the arrest.

A split second later I was there beside them, and grabbed the woman in a choke hold. I would've snatched the chick off but she had a grip on Maritza's hair. All I could do was apply pressure. "Let 'er go! Right fucking now!" I demanded through clenched teeth.

But this woman was wild, no different than any one of the doped-up men that we've arrested from time to time. I squeezed harder now, and I didn't care if I broke the woman's neck.

THE INCIDENT UP on Gun Hill Road turned out to be more involved, with more paperwork to write up, than most other calls we've addressed. Number one, I choked the woman into unconsciousness. So the Internal Affairs Division as well as the Civilian Review people got all up in the mix. Of course, with the history of NYPD being what it is (Amadou Diallo, Anthony Baez, Abner Louima—better known in the department as "the execution, the choke-out and the plunger stick up the ass"), there would always be the claims of police brutality to answer. The slightest thing would mean more paperwork explaining our actions. More questions to answer.

Second, regardless of the woman needing medical attention and being brought to the hospital, she
was still under arrest for assaulting an officer and
for obstruction of justice.

To add fuel to the flames, Nancy's boss, Mr.
Brown, was indeed in the office trailer, only he was
also very much unconscious. It turned out that
Nancy's boyfriend had caught the two (the boss
and the office assistant) in a romantic embrace, after which he punched out the elder Mr. Brown. So,
not only did Nancy Grimes have to be brought to
Montefiore, but her boss, Mr. Brown, did, too.

The pile of paperwork that Maritza and I had to
complete carried us well into the six o'clock hour,
when most office workers might be having an
after-work drink, or they might be at home with
the family. This is the life of a police officer.

"You think the judge will give the guy bail?" I
asked Maritza after we finally finished two days'
worth of documents.

"I can't say. I hope not, considering how
Grimes' face looked. The D.A. is gonna make sure
the judge sees photos of her at the arraignment.
He's gonna show how the boyfriend is a danger to
her or to anyone else," she replied.

"But what if she can't post bail? Would there
still be—"

"I guess it's up to the judge. The good thing is,
the magistrate on duty tomorrow is Judge Flowers.

She's notorious for lockin' men up if there's evidence of abuse and battery."

"Okay. I remember her speaking at this year's National Black Caucus."

"Right. But she protects Latinos and whites, too."

"Hmmm . . . that sounds like someone we should all study . . . maybe follow her lead."

I threw that subtle hint to Maritza as she dropped me off at my place. I didn't wanna hear shit-else about police work, the local news, nothin'. As a matter of fact, I was quietly praying that April had fixed one of her good ole home-cooked meals. That would earn her more brownie points in my book than anything else she's done while living with me.

April is such a quiet soul, too. She allows me my space and, no, she hasn't let on about her boyfriend yet. But I know she's seeing somebody, with her glowin'-ass cheeks. To tell you the truth, I didn't much care about who her man was, as long as she was happy. Yes, I was curious as hell, but no, I didn't need to know all the inside stuff. I suppose she'll eventually tell all.

"Well, well, well," I said as I came in the door. Coco Puff wasn't as excited these days; she wasn't jumpin' up at me as soon as I got home. Of course that has to be April's warm affection at work. Makin my dog all comfy-cozy.

"All dressed up with someplace to go?"

"Oh—hey, Sissy. I made your favorite. Barbecue chicken. It's keeping warm in the oven . . ."

I could already smell it, and the aroma did won-
ders to my senses. "Okay, so much for the food.
Now, how about a clue as to where you're headed
on this dreamy Tuesday night?"

April was in her bathrobe, blowing on a freshly
painted fingernail. "You're not keeping tabs on me,
are you, Sissy?"

"Actually, aside from plain ole curiosity, I'm a
little envious. It looks like you've landed what I've
been wanting for the longest. The satisfaction with
no strings attached. I just hope you get all that you
deserve, and that he doesn't disrespect you."

"Oh, Sissy. Don't get so deep. I'm not fornicating or anything. We've hardly kissed. But I appreciate your blessings. Believe me, when the marriage
proposal comes, from him or anyone, you'll be the
first . . . well . . . the second to know."

I smiled, then April and I shared a friendly embrace. There went that strange feeling again, as if
some of what she was experiencing (the love, the
anticipation) was being transferred or exchanged.
"You promise?"

"I promise, two times over. Now go get yourself
changed up, dinner's waiting."

I went to the oven, pulled open the door to take a
long whiff to hold me till later. Then I ran a hot bath
with oils and crystals to help my body relax. A half
hour later, while I was soaking and inhaling the

menthol fumes, I heard the front door close. It was an eye-opener, the reality that April was going out to do Lord knows what, with Lord knows who, and that I was left to cope with my after-work loneliness.

Since I was alone now, and since Coco Puff was watching *Animal Planet*, I went for it. I relaxed a little more and gave special attention to myself, caressing my own curves, my arms and legs, my breasts and nipples; and then I spread my legs some, cocked them, and eased my two fingers inside of my wet hungry folds. I could always count on bringing myself to orgasm if I ever had the urge. Since I've been alone for so long, I generally get by without satisfaction for three or four weeks. But usually right after my period, a girl's gotta have it. Sometimes I imagine myself with a movie star, sometimes with an NBA player.

But I also have this recurring fantasy about taking a drive one night along I-95. I'd see a hitchhiker and stop to pick him up. It was always a man, and always a different person.

"Where you headed, big boy?"

"Anywhere you wanna go, baby," the hitchhiker would answer. Most times the guy would be a little scruffy with a couple of days' facial hair, and he'd be a little funky from walking so far for so long. But I didn't care. These were the experiences that mattered to me. It was what I wanted. No strings attached.

With some hitchhikers, I talked them into having

a drink with me. With others, I let them influence me with their gift of gab. I'd let them believe I was a woman who could be easily manipulated. And in my dreams, in the tub or in my bed, they sure did manipulate me.

One guy used my handcuffs to hold me down and greased up a wooden baseball bat. Then he pushed it up into me real rough as I cried and resisted. Another guy who chained me down (not cuffed me, chained me!) put his ear to my pussy and listened to me for a whole hour. In the meantime, he had a damned conversation with my pussy like this was a place to make a long-distance call! Another guy fucked me with his foot. One after the other. There were freakier and freakier hitchhikers. That is, if you'd call sitting on my face freaky.

And the thing is, this one guy seemed so normal. He even had on a three-piece suit when I picked him up. What he was doing out on I-95 so late at night beats me. But it was all so romantic until we got naked in a no-name hotel off the highway. He asked me to fulfill his fantasy and said that he'd fulfill mine. And I believed him. I was a little shocked when he asked to sit on my face. I mean, after all, we just met. But I still went ahead with it. As real as this felt, it was still imaginary. And besides, it was my fantasy after all.

"You're not gonna suffocate me, are you?"

"Nah, of course not! I need you alive so I can reciprocate."

And I thought, Ooohh-wee . . . re-cip-ro-cate. Such big words from such an important-looking man. It made me ask, "Why were you out there hitchhiking, anyway?"

"My car broke down," he snapped back. And I believed him again. "Now, get ready," he said, apparently wanting to get moving. He climbed over my naked body. His dick was short like a worm, and uncircumcised, too.

I wanted to be sick, and I was so glad he didn't want me to suck it. But at the same time I was excited. Moist like some kind of gooey fruit. He lowered his ass onto my face. He rubbed himself up and down against my forehead, nose and lips. He ordered me to lick him, to suck him, to eat him. And I obeyed, knowing that this guy would blow my mind in just a few minutes. If this was all he wanted, for a perfect stranger to lick his asshole, then my fantasy was about to rock his world.

When he was done, his ass thoroughly cleaned under my experienced tongue, the man got up to go to the bathroom. He stayed in there for at least ten minutes.

"Sorry to keep you," he said. And I could smell the fumes behind him. "Now where were we?"

"Where were we? I thought I was finished. I thought it was my turn," I said as he climbed over me.

"A couple more minutes, baby. Just finish the job and I swear I'll turn your ass inside out."

I hesitated, but he gave me a gentle shove back on the bed. He straddled me again and lowered his ass onto my face. Wide-eyed and utterly shocked, I realized that this man had just taken a shit and hadn't wiped himself! On purpose! I struggled, but the weight of him on my limbs was impossible to escape. Plus, he already had his ass painting my face as it had earlier. UGH! My entire face smelled of shit, forehead, nose and mouth. There was a point, since I was already in too deep, that I went on and made the best of it. If this was his fantasy, so be it. I've been through worse things. I think.

"Are you quite finished?" I asked the stranger, still unaware of his name.

"Yeah," he said, and pulled out a cigarette.

"I don't smoke," I said, hoping he'd get the hint-hint, clue-clue.

"Oh," he muttered, but continued to take his drags. "So, ah . . . what was it that you wanted done?"

I took a deep breath, figuring that this must be where things took a turn for the best. "Well . . . for starters, I wanted to have my toes sucked . . ."

The hitchhiker began laughing amidst the smoky swirls.

"And then . . . well, I've always wanted to have my underarms licked . . ."

"Underarms! Ha ha ha . . ." He couldn't stop laughing.

"And then I'm going to give you a golden shower."

There was this silence. He became still. Then he broke into a laugh that I swore they heard two or three hotel rooms down.

"What's so funny?" I asked with my hands on my hips.

"This!" he said. I saw his fist coming at me and everything went black.

I'VE HAD THAT dream at least a dozen times and I still can't get to my end of the fantasy.

# APRIL

STUART WAS MINE the moment I caught him with his secret admirer basket. I mean, I'm a child of the Lord and all, but I'm not stupid. This was a once in a lifetime opportunity. It's not my problem if he walked out on his family, or that Sissy was denied a father. I'm sure Sissy can get along without. Shoot. She *has* been getting along! She's got a successful career going, she's secure in her own home, pit bull at the ready. Meanwhile, look at me—I'm a freelancer, living hand-to-mouth, praying on jobs and hoping I get them. No home, so I have to be someone's housemate.

I believe in God, and yes, Jesus is my Lord and Savior, but my clock is ticking! I want to live and love now, not in any afterlife. And besides, I know what the Bible tells me, but what if there is no afterlife? Nobody really knows. It's not like someone went to visit and came back to tell us all what

it's like. We're all just having faith in a book—
God's Word, we've all been calling it. But it was
man who put the book together! Not only that,
there are so many thousands and thousands of
books that came *before* the Bible. Hello???

So I'm supposed to have lived this life humble
and sexless. For what? So I can go through the
pearly gates and claim that I've been "righteous"
for at least half my life? I think not! Shoot. Everybody else seems to be living it up with a man in
their lives. So this might have been my calling, for
me to run into this man. Something told me that
this was a now-or-never decision. Maybe it was
God talking.

I suggested to Stuart that he go through me to
get closer to his daughter. The idea turned out to be
a winner. For me. Number one, he always paid the
bill for our dinners. Number two, dinner meant
that our conversations would be intimate, where I
could really pick his brain. And, number three, I
could make an honest decision to go forward with
this. If it was worth sinning, I could follow
through. If something felt funny, I could back out,
and all under the presumption of this so-called "investigation."

We were downtown at B. Smith's when Stuart
asked if he was getting any closer to meeting Sissy.

"Well, Mr. Dickerson—"

"I hate when you do that, April. You make me
sound so old," he said.

"Well then, why can't you honor my request? I asked that you not bring up Sissy's name unless I did. I'm still trying to figure you out. Trying to see if you're sincere. That's the way we said we'd do it, right?"

"Yes, yes . . . of course. I'm sorry, I just—"

"I'm trying to get to know you as a human being. I need to know what kind of man you are. All different layers. Any deadbeat dad can walk back into his child's life and claim this and claim that. But the truth lies far beyond all the words. That simple action—'Daddy's home'—heck no. I'm not gonna let my friend fall for that. In fact, she told me that she won't fall for it. She told me to scrutinize you until I see your real juice. And if you don't want to go along with what I—what she wants, then I can leave right now."

I was prepared to go. I threw down my napkin and everything. But I could already see how the man was falling for my act. Eyes watering and everything. I knew I had him with the "deadbeat dad" statement. But I was sure he was sold on the "she won't fall for it" line.

"Okay, okay. Please, sit. I . . . no, I didn't mean it like that. Please, have a seat, April. I'm so sorry . . ." Now his tears began to stream down his cheeks. He was choking up.

"I just don't know what you want me to do. Do you want my blood? I'll give you my blood. Do you want me to chop off my right hand? I'll do that.

I just . . . I need your help, April. My life isn't complete without . . . Oh my God."

This was getting too sloppy. I had seen enough of this side of him. The sensitivity.

"It's okay, Stuart." I came around to his side of the table and put my arm around him. We were hugging cheek-to-cheek. "It's gonna be just fine."

After dinner I suggested that we go to the Times Square Arcade. In a sense, I expressed to him that these activities (dinner, movies, and so forth) might be a good show of how a daddy might treat his daughter after being away so long. Stuart understood and seemed ready for the different video games; we battled each other in a handful of them. I swear he let me win every time. At the pinball machine, I told him I was new to the game. That it seemed like something for old folks. At one point, the silver ball kept getting by without me catching it at all with the little rubber flippers.

Stuart came to the rescue. "Lemme show you," he said. And he came up behind me, his body touching me and his hands over mine. Meanwhile, his lips were this close to my cheek. I pushed my hair behind my ear with my neck tilted some so that he could see over my shoulder.

"See, the trick is to anticipate where the silver ball is gonna . . . hit the . . . umph!" Stuart let out a grunt and the silver ball was smacked back up into the obstacles, bells and whistles under the glass of the pinball game. But my mind was elsewhere, too shaken by the feel of him rubbing, bumping and thrusting his lower body against my behind. The electricity that shot through me was awesome.

And then he did it again. I resisted from jumping and so felt the gentle force of the bulge . . . his bulge against my butt. Oh my God! I squeezed my eyes closed as Stuart became absorbed in the game, smacking the ball here and there. I wasn't sure if he knew how much the friction was affecting me. I couldn't tell if this was intentional. My hope was that it was. But then, what else did he have in mind? I played it by ear and said nothing. And in an arcade full of wanderers, we might as well have been invisible. In our own world.

IN STUART'S AUDI, all was deathly silent on the way back uptown. I sat in the passenger's seat, as close to the door as possible, staring out of the window at nothing and everything. It was one of those occasions where I couldn't tell if the trees, traffic lights and street signs were moving, or if it was me alone. I think this was what they called an altered state.

"Please don't say anything to Sissy, April. I'm not a bad man. It's just that . . . well . . . you're so damned beautiful . . ."

And young, I added in my mind.

"And I'm still a man, April. A single man. A lonely, single man . . ."

And you're my best friend's father.

"I guess I couldn't resist," he said.

And I guess I liked it, I thought.

"This was all a mistake. I knew it. Seeing you so much . . . trying to fix the past with my daughter. It was all wrong. I must seem like the worst man in the world to you. A failure."

"Stuart?"

"Y-yes?"

"Stop babbling and take me home."

"Uh—okay." He adjusted his attention to the road.

"Your home," I clarified. And there it was, that promise that women don't usually allude to. "Give them a hint that they can taste the milk, and they'll come and raid the whole friggin' farm," Momma used to say. Stuart's head never moved. He kept his eyes fixed on some infinite vanishing point beyond his windshield. In the meantime, I pretended to bite my thumbnail, but in fact, I was sucking my thumb.

I can't believe I'm doing this.

STUART DICKERSON LIVED on Mary Street, just below the start of the #2 line. As much as this was the inner city, where houses were seemingly squeezed in beside one another, it was still a humble residential zone where folks kept their homes presentable, if not attractive.

"How long have you lived here?" I wanted to know.

"It feels like my whole life. But really, about fifteen years. The neighbors are okay. Everybody keeps to themselves. Nothin' too crazy."

"Are you the only white man on the block?" I asked boldly.

Stuart froze in his tracks, just before he unlocked his front door. Was it something I said?

"Now what in God's name ever gave you that idea? That I was white?"

"Well, your skin is white," I said matter-of-factly.

"Wow. You in the younger generation sure have a lot to learn. And for your information, dear April, I am not white."

I was stunned. I quietly followed him into his single-family home, out from under the late night stars and the half moon. The first thing I noticed was a pine fragrance. Whether it was the wood paneling, the furnishings or something artificial, I couldn't say. It sure didn't seem artificial.

"Smells good," I said.

"Thanks. But I always thought it needed a woman's touch."

"You come across this in your real estate work?"

"Oh yeah. I see a lot of houses. A whole lot. And this one, well, it made sense. Not too big and not too small, ya know? Tucked into a residential neighborhood, but not too far from the local pizza shop, grocery store and train station."

"Hmmm . . . I noticed."

"May I take your jacket?" he asked, and I let him. Then I meandered further into his living room.

"Please make yourself at home. Can I get you a drink? Or do you saved women have certain rules?"

I smirked, ready to read him. But instead I said, "We're allowed to drink responsibly, Stuart, for your information. And I'll have a Harvey's on ice, thank you very much." I rolled my eyes, keeping things lighthearted. Stuart melted away with a somewhat guilty expression before we continued our chat. I sat on one of the four stools by the bar, while he performed as bartender. The TV was on, BET's music videos providing the background soundtrack to the scene. I was able to see him in his essence now, even if it was for some (so-called) research for my friend Sissy. But now I wondered just how long we would be best friends, considering.

"So shweethart . . . what's a pretty girl like you doin' in a rusty ole place like this?" Stuart's impersonation sounded familiar.

"Lemme guess," I said, "Frank Sinatra?"

"Sinatra? What do you know about Frank Sinatra?" The way he asked that had me feeling somewhat embarrassed.

"Oh, ahh, nothing, really. I was just guessing."

Stuart chuckled. "Actually, it was Humphrey Bogart. Do you watch them ole black-and-white films?"

"Not really. I used to watch the old black spoit . . ." My memory escaped me.

"Blaxploitation films?" he asked.

"Yeah. That's it. Before I was saved I would watch, like, Pam Grier, plus I liked those ones with Bill Cosby and Sidney Poitier."

*"Let's Do It Again."*

"Yeah. And *Uptown Saturday Night*," I added.

"When they ran up in the club and robbed everyone, and took the lottery ticket? Had 'em strip naked? Oooh, baby."

"That one was okay," I said. "But my favorite was *A Piece of the Action*. That had a better plot to me."

"Agreed," Stuart said and passed me my Harvey's. Before I sipped he raised his glass. "Shall we toast?"

"Okay; to what?"

"To new beginnings . . . fresh starts."

"Mmm . . . I like that," I said. And we tapped glasses.

"So . . . me being the bartender and all . . . how about sharing some of your blues with me? You already know mine."

"Ahh ha haa . . . good one," I said with my soft laugh. "Well, I wasn't fortunate like the other girls. My daddy died when I was ten. Momma was admitted to an institution . . ."

"You're kidding."

"Nope. I went to a foster family, but I really felt all alone in the world. No blood to claim."

"I'm so sorry to hear that."

"Don't be sorry. Just listen!" I heard myself yell at him, but I didn't know where it came from. Stuart was frozen in disbelief, leaning on the counter only a few feet away.

"See, it was this black hole I was living in. A bottomless, black hole. And year after year, I felt I was falling deeper. No-good boyfriends . . . deeper. No father to give me hugs on my birthday . . . deeper. No daddy to say Happy Father's Day to . . . deeper. Drugs . . . deeper. Sexual encounters . . . oh, my . . . it was so bad." I sighed and I felt as if I drifted away as I spoke.

"Are you okay, April?"

"Don't touch me!" I barked and snatched my wrist away.

"You could've been there for me, Daddy. You could've at least shown your face before you died. You could've been there to pray with me . . . could've asked God to tell me things . . . could've boxed with Jesus . . . could've had my children . . ." I screamed after saying all of this. It calmed me. I was in space. Lost. I wasn't sure what I'd said . . . or what I was saying. Stuart's eyes were wide with surprise. He had backed up away from the bar, almost dropping his drink.

"Stuart? Are you okay?" I was calm now. "I didn't go off again, did I?" I got up from the stool and came around to where he was. He seemed to want to avoid me like the plague.

"April, what's happening to you? Do you hear what you're saying?"

"To be honest? No. I trip sometimes. Space out, ya know? Like, I feel possessed when I least expect it . . ." I was close to him now, and I felt we were friends enough for a hug, at least. I closed my eyes and put my arms around him, pulling myself into his warmth. I felt the apprehension at first. But shortly thereafter I was swallowed by his compassion, his understanding and his, well . . . this was comfortable. Too comfortable. I shivered with so many ideas running through my mind. For sure, I'd crossed the line. The threshold of sin. If not physically, then surely mentally.

"Don't send me home," I pleaded. "I know I've been a bad girl."

"April, I'm afraid this is moving a little too fast for—"

Before Stuart could say another word, I glued my lips to his, filling the whole of his mouth with my tongue. I had lost my mind. I was crazed with denial and desire all at once. This was defiantly ungodly, but it felt so darned good. Could I have my voids filled by this man? Could he make up for what had been missing in my life for so long? I remembered the feeling I had when I accepted Jesus Christ as my Lord and Savior. Ever since that day, that high, nothing had ever given me such ecstasy.

Not until now. Now my body felt so good all over. Tingling from head to toe, and everywhere in between. Everywhere. I didn't ever want to let go of this sensation. And however possible, I wanted more of it. I needed more of it. Suddenly, something made me pull away. "Oh God!" I cried and tripped over one of the bar stools, falling back to the floor. I found myself looking up; things were spinning. The walls, light fixtures, and furniture. All this new atmosphere made for an indoor cyclone, with me at the center.

"April? April! Oh damn . . ." I felt hands lifting me, then arms carrying me, then the softness of a couch giving underneath me. Stuart's face was there, except it was slightly blurred.

I saw Sissy's face, her tears falling; she was asking me, Why are you stealing my daddy? I thought you were my best friend. Beside Sissy's face was Jesus. And Jesus was a white man, like all of those images I saw as a child. And now Jesus was saying, Stay with Me, April. Don't go. I need you to spread the word . . . I need you to be righteous and wholesome. And now there was Stuart, stroking my forehead, asking me if I was okay . . . if I could hear his voice . . . if I was hurt . . .

"Things are spinning, I . . . oh, my head."

"I'm calling a doctor," Stuart said.

"No," I said, clutching his arm. "I just need some attention, Stuart." I pulled his arm, urging him to come closer. "I just need you," I said, smiling.

Finally, this man who was old enough to be my father was lowering himself onto me, clinging to me like some heavy bodysuit. Our mouths connected once again and our tongues made every effort at trading places. The shivering I had been feeling was gone, replaced by spasms between my legs. Between my folds.

I sighed.

I pulled him closer.

I pressed myself up into him, meeting his force with my own. When I had a chance to take a breath, I said, "Would you be my daddy?"

Stuart made a strange face, as if at a loss for words. Instead of speaking he took my mouth again. I guessed that to be my answer. We went on like this for some time, the giving and taking.

"Wait a minute," Stuart took a moment to say. "Was that whole trip and fall a trap? Did I just fall for a trick?"

"Of course not, Stuart. Why would I trick you? How would I trick you? As wise and experienced as you are?" Stuart made a face, doubting me. I said, "Oh God . . . I'm getting dizzy again. Kiss me!" And I pulled him again, plugging my tongue back into his mouth. It didn't matter that I tricked him. I was getting what I wanted. A daddy. A lover.

We were playful and silly on the couch until things turned serious. He had opened my shirt to expose my breasts. I had learned the shape of his erection, eventually slipping it out of hiding. I was laying half-naked on my back. And while my lover went on kissing and devouring my breasts, my

eyes cut over to the television—The BET Awards
were on; G-Unit was performing, rapping about
how they were on fire. So was I. Stuart cradled my
body now, close enough for us to continue kissing.

I convinced him to take me into the bedroom
and in the semidarkness I felt his experienced
hands undress me all the way in a delicate manner.
I was his gift-wrapped virgin, ready to learn. He
was my teacher, but I intended to impress and
overwhelm him at each opportunity.

Soon both of us were naked. I took the opportunity to explore Stuart's slender figure, his muscles
and his face. I took his fingers in my mouth one at
a time, showing him how naughty I could be. How
naughty I intended to be.

While he lay on his back, I experimented with
his pecs, nibbling at his nipples to make them hard
like my own. I made a trail down the center of his
chest and abdomen until my tongue was grazing
through his grassy pubic area.

"Is April making Daddy happy? Does Daddy
like it when I . . . do this? "How 'bout . . . this? I'm
a bad girl," I said.

Still, mixed thoughts were pushing and pulling
at my conscience. Some inner voice was telling
me: It has to be right by God, April, and you
shouldn't be with him until marriage . . . no more
of that fornicating. That sounded like the April I
knew. But the April tonight was singing another
tune. This was the April wearing her angel eyes as

she looked up at Stuart. This was the April that could always appear to be innocent, yet underneath the mask, she wanted to sin, sin, sin. And that's what April wanted to do now. Sin. She wanted to sin something awful.

"Relax," I told him. "Make believe it's Father's Day and this is your gift. From me, to you, Daddy," I said in this girlish voice. I propped myself back against the pillows on Stuart's bed, and pulled him slowly into my mouth, smoothing my lips and tongue along his throbbing penis until I could take no more. It was eventually all in my mouth so that I could feel every bit of my gums touching him, making him at home, snug inside of me. Yes, yes, yes! Let me have it all.

Stuart grunted and moaned above me, so I had to be doing everything right. That was one thing that bothered me, whether or not I could make him happy, or at least satisfied. Of course he must've experienced so many exciting women in his lifetime. I wasn't going for the "I can't find a woman" act. Stuart was no ugly duckling. In fact, I could imagine him being a *GQ* model in his younger years. I'm a lonely single man, April. Yeah, Stuart. Sure you are.

While Stuart continued to feed me, I stayed busy with my tongue and cheeks, feeling my new love squirm and twitch. I figured Stuart to be a busy ladies' man, probably juggling them at his convenience. But now they'd have me to deal with. Call me motormouth with my aggressive oral sex, but don't ever call me a stranger to this man. I knew that I could sure give Stuart something that no other woman could provide. Something richer. I could satisfy him as a lover on one hand, and I could pretend to be his daughter whenever he needed it. You need a shoulder massage, Daddy? Can I get your slippers? How about a nice home-cooked meal like Mommy used to make? Whatever he had, I'd serve him. Just a minute, Daddy. I'm coming! Yes. I could fill the emptiness left by him missing Sissy——missing his real daughter's love.

As all of those thoughts were running around in my head, Stuart's hands were busy kneading my scalp. He didn't notice that I'd slipped my wig off, since the lights weren't on, but none of that mattered now! This scalp massage was *incredible*! I couldn't help thinking that he was satisfying my head, while I was satisfying his. And the more he dug into my nappy wool, the more aggressive I was with the jerking, with both hands busy and desperate.

I was sure Stuart was lying to me about being lonely; but then, I suppose everybody has lies to tell. Oh well. I felt his hand and fingers combing through my hair as my head bobbed up and down. I allowed my mouth to water, to become that soft, slippery hole for his penis to get lost in. I wanted him to feel welcome, hoping that this was as good for him as it was for me. Not wanting to be the to-tal bad girl, and maybe milking him until he begged for mercy, I eased my lips off of him and flicked my tongue on his sensitive tip.

"N-n-n-no . . . d-dd-d-don't," Stuart begged, urging me to stop teasing. His wish was my command.

"Can I sit on it, Daddy?"

It wasn't the type of question that required an answer. I acted automatically, raising up to lower my body for a perfect fit. I ooohed and ahhed and raised my arms over my head, folding them behind the back of my neck. It was only seconds into the act, but I already felt complete. Like, this is the way things are supposed to be.

Stuart's hands kneaded my breasts with soft power while I gyrated in his lap.

"Oh Daddy . . . you're so big inside of me," I said, with half-closed eyes, my head rolling . . . swaying to the music. Stuart was like a strong saxophone filling me with song . . . a drum that corresponded with my pounding heart. I was a frail violin being transformed into an electric guitar . . . a piano whose keys he came to know personally. Along with my sighs and cries, along with his growls and heavy panting, the bedroom was a soundstage with the two of us serving as the full-string orchestra of passion. Of lust.

"Oh, Daddy! Yes, Daddy!" I carried on, bouncing now, wanting more of him although he was already fully engorged inside of me. "Give it to me, Daddy! Yes! Yes! Yessss!" I shook with this, my second orgasm, and still, I craved more.

"Talk dirty to me . . . make me your whore," I said, slumped over against his chest. "Treat me like your bad girl."

"You are a bad girl," he said, and finally I felt Stuart pushing up under me.

Thank you, God! It's not just me! He wants me!

Then he said, "Now turn your ass over. Get on your hands and knees. Now! I'm gonna punish you."

Now that I was positioned doggy-style, Stuart took my hips in his firm, knowing hands and pushed his erection into me from behind.

"You like that? Huh? You like that, you little slut? You want a daddy so bad? Huh?" Stuart managed to growl his words as he thrust himself into me again and again. "Well I'll tell you what . . . take this . . . uunh . . . big . . . aargh . . . dick . . ." His hard penis was almost too much to bear, banging every inch of my walls. I felt as if I was some kind of tough meat being tenderized by a hammer.

"Oh yes, Daddy! Give it to me. Yes! Yes! I am a slut! I'm your slut. Punish me . . . punish me . . ." My voice trailed off in a kind of dying shrill. My body was like a lifeless crash-test dummy, being pushed and banged and twisted and tossed, recklessly, until Stuart finally let out a he-man's yowl.

"Oh shit!" he yelled. He withdrew his penis, spewing his sperm on my legs, and then fell onto my back as though life had been vacuumed out of him in one mad rush.

I felt weird when it ended. As if time stood still.

I needed to be held and told that this man was right. That things would be okay from now on. I wanted this to mean that my dream had come true. But Stuart just lay there on my back, staring up at the ceiling. I continued to shiver as I turned to look at my lover, my Daddy, my everything. I didn't think about Sissy. I didn't think about God. I just thought about Stuart. Stuart and April. I wondered if we were now one. If we were now the center of our own world. I thought of security, of affection unmatched and of spending every waking hour with this man! My man.

No longer was I concerned with our age difference, or the different lives we'd led. I wanted Stuart to tell me that the past was no more, and that life began right here and now.

I VISITED STUART three or four times since that first night. And it seemed to me that he became more and more insensitive each time. Cocky, even. More taking than giving. But I was okay with that. We had one full day of what he called "orientation," where I was made to clean his house, from the spiderwebs behind the couches to the urine stains along the sides of his toilets. I had to beat carpets and wash windows and clean the oven. I did all of this with an apron on. Only an apron. After washing the dirty buildup in his tub, I was finally told to bathe. While I was in the tub, Stuart came into the bathroom and sat on the toilet just to talk, or so it seemed.

"Did I work you too hard?" he asked.

"Oh, no, Stuart. Are you kidding?" I had a joyous smile across my face. "I'm here to serve you. Whatever you want. Whatever you need. It's my pleasure, really."

"Your pleasure."

"Sure," I said sincerely. "I'm making up for some things. I would've done this for my own daddy. So why not do it for you? I look at it as sort of . . . boot camp. Like you said, orientation."

Stuart nodded and seemed to look through me, as though I were transparent.

Then I said, "It's also for you to be comfortable with me. I want you to take me, Stuart. If this is my big audition—my test—I want to pass with flying colors. I want to show you, prove to you that I can satisfy all your needs. All of them."

"All of them?"

"Mmm-hmm," I said, a girlish blush across my face.

"Okay, then . . ." Stuart said. He got up and approached the bathtub. He loosened his belt, unzipped his fly and let his penis hang out. We hadn't had sex yet, not on this particular day, and I had been wondering when I could satisfy him. I guess it was now.

"Suck my dick, April."

"I thought you'd never ask, Daddy."


ON ANOTHER VISIT, Stuart said we were gonna play games. Night games, he called them.

"Oooh . . . I like this already," I said as he tied a thick rope around my wrists and my ankles, and stretched me out on his bed. "Do I get blindfolded, too?" Stuart froze for a moment. Maybe he couldn't believe that I was all for this. But I was all for it.

"Yeah. Sure," he said. And he tied a scarf around my head so that I couldn't see. If this were anyone else, I might've rejected this. But there was such a bond between Stuart and me. I was the daughter he never had and the lover who would never leave him. And Stuart? Stuart was my daddy. He could punish me, love me and bark orders at me, and it would be okay. Because now I realized, that's what daddies did.

Now that I was bound and gagged, Stuart dripped hot wax on me, causing me to shriek until the sting of it felt familiar. Until it didn't hurt any-more. After the wax, he talked dirty to me until I felt his semen squirt on my face and breasts. It was icky, but I kind of liked it. It made me moist and excited. And to top that off, after his hearty grunt and the last drops that fell to my body, Stuart sprayed hot urine all over my neck, breasts and lower region. I was mortified at first, having never done that before. Thank God I kept my mouth closed, because I couldn't imagine the taste of it— only that it would surely be worse then the smelly fumes were.

Stuart eventually untied me and told me to pose

for him; some really awkward positions, too. I
didn't know he wanted to take Polaroid photos.
But, whatever. I think he took three or four rolls—
maybe sixty pictures in all. I didn't ask (and didn't
care) what they were for. If he asked for it, it was
okay by me. But I couldn't guess why he wanted a
handful of photos of me naked, with sperm, urine
and wax all over me. Surely I could look a lot pret-
tier for Daddy.

ON ANOTHER NIGHT Stuart had me bent over his
kitchen table and he snatched off my pants—and
my panties—and stuck me in my rear end. But always, there were spankings or other kinds of
bondage that had me twisted like a pretzel.

So far, our relationship was a blast!

# RIVER

**IF I THOUGHT** I could get away with it, I'd write a book about all the ways I've killed a man. I'd go on a publicity campaign in ten or twenty of the largest cities, and I'd do all of the interviews I could fit within twenty-four hours. Newspapers, magazines, television and radio would eat it up. Every news-maker, broadcaster and publisher in the nation would want to get at me. I'd wear a mask and alter my voice so that I'd never be recognized, then I'd explain one or two killings in all their meticulous detail. I'd tell them how I do things, how guns and knives were just plain boring.

"That's for the common killer," I'd say. "I like to kill men in creative ways. Ways that will be memorable to me and to the cops who investigate. Something extraordinary for the world at large."

"Wow," the newscaster would say. "Could you

share a couple of those encounters with us? I mean, what do you consider creative?"

And I'd pretend to be naive about the question, like I don't know they're trying to get down to the nitty-gritty. But that's exactly what I wanted. I wanted to get down to the nitty-gritty.

"Well, first lemme tell you about my victims."

"Okay. Whatever you like."

"See, the man's gotta be the scum of the earth. He's gotta deserve what I'm about to do to him . . . that doesn't mean I won't kill an honest, kind-hearted gentleman. I don't discriminate when it comes to killing. And by the way, I have done that."

"Done what? Discriminate?"

"Killed someone who seemed honest. Good-natured. It's just . . . well, they happened to get in the way when I was finishing off the scum."

"Oh, I get it. No loose ends left."

"Exactly. But to stay focused, most of the men I've killed have been deserving."

"And, dare I ask, how many of those deserving types have you killed?"

"I lost count after twenty-five. It's almost like driving a car for the first time—ohh, this is my sixth time; ohh, today I drove at night; tomorrow I'm driving on the parkway. It's the same with killing. Once you've done it so many times, I guess it becomes routine."

"Oh, my. Twenty-five . . ."

"Twenty-five plus."

"You must be the foremost expert on the subject."

"I'd say. Especially since—knock on wood—I haven't been caught," I'd tell the world.

"So, let's get down to the details. Tell us what is considered creative killing."

"Well . . . let's say you're a man. Maybe you're a pimp who owns a dozen women, and all day long they sell their bodies just to bring you money."

"Okay. I'll try," the broadcaster would say with a strange expression.

"See, this one's easy, because all I'd need to do is dress up and look real pretty—like a girl who just finished high school. Ya know . . . fresh meat . . ."

"O—kay."

"I'd lie to you and say I want to show you how good I am, I want to show you that I can be your biggest moneymaker."

The newscaster would squirm in the seat as I said this. The cameraman would salivate, too.

"And then, of course, you'd wanna test me out. You'd expect to have your way with me."

"I see," the newsman would say, halfway under my spell.

"I'd get you to take me someplace intimate . . . real private, like your home, or maybe a cabin in the woods. Somewhere that a whole lot of yelling and screaming wouldn't be heard. And if that wasn't possible, I'd just bring a roll of duct tape with me."

"Duct tape."

"Mmm-hmm . . . duct tape and Valium."

"Whoa."

"Of course we'd have a drink—which I'd spike—when we got settled, and you would drink, because I'd seduce you so well. I'd be sexy and sensual and I'd make you want me more than you've ever wanted any woman."

Silence from the newscaster.

"Once the Valium set in and you were under sedation, I'd tie you up and take your shoes and socks off."

"Just the shoes and socks?"

"That's all. Then, before you came around to full consciousness, I'd already be ripping your toenails off one by one. And I'd pull them back enough so that just about the whole nail came off . . ." The newscaster would cringe and shake at the thought, but I'd continue. "Of course there would be blood everywhere, and you'd eventually piss your pants."

"H-how, may I ask, would you rip these, ahh, toenails off?"

"With my pliers," I'd reply matter-of-factly. "See, I have a few tools I take along for the job. The needlenose pliers are just the beginning. The wire cutters would be next."

"Oh my . . . what in the world would you do with those?"

"I'd probably have to tie you down to keep you from moving. Then I'd open your nostrils—give you some larger holes where your nose once was. After the nose, I'd clip your eyelids from your face. This way you'd never shut your eyes. Even after you're buried. After the nose and the eyelids, I'd go for your ears. I'd clip them off with these shears I have; they're real heavy-duty, with thick rubber handles. If you weren't unconscious by now, I'd use forceps to pull out your eyeballs. I wouldn't just leave them hanging either. I'd go back to the wire cutters, I'd cut the optical nerves and I'd stuff both eyeballs in your mouth. I got that idea from a book I read called *The Breast Factory*."

"Uh . . . I'm sorry. We, uh, we need to go to a commercial break. We'll be back with more of this woman who claims to be behind the Pink Heart murders right after these messages."

Never could my press tour take place. Never. I've dreamed about it over and again, but there's no way I could pull it off without one of those television personalities venturing to be a hero. They'd pretend to look out for my best interest . . . they'd promise me this and that. But, at the end of the day, I'd be in handcuffs on my way to death row.

The book and publicity campaign were some of my better dreams. The nightmares were unbearable—so much so that I'd have to wake up and go after my next victim.

I recently heard about a situation that took place at a used car lot on Gun Hill Road. A woman had the daylights beaten out of her by her boyfriend in front of a group of bystanders who just plain didn't give a fuck. They watched the assault and (probably) cheered just like the audiences do at wrestling matches. The police came and arrested the boyfriend, and the judge let him out. A week later, the guy beat the woman again. Again, she didn't press charges.

I'm no Wonder Woman, on a daily mission to stick up for the abused women of the Bronx, but I sure wouldn't mind gettin' a piece of him. And I'm just the person for the job.

I like to kill. I like to kill certain men. And I don't think this is a problem or an illness as much as it's a passion. I wanna massacre the mothafuckas. Slimeballs must die for what they do. They're allowed to beat on women, rape women; even if they desert women, that's a man who's good enough for me to add to my own list of victims.

It didn't take long for me to find out that this guy's name was Freddie Cox, and that he lived on Laconia Avenue with his girlfriend, Nancy Grimes, who I realized was the very woman he frequently beat the shit out of. I also found out that the two had a child together. But I didn't care.

As far as I was concerned, my next victim was already lined up, just as a duck is for a hunter. Freddie, the duck. And like some headstrong detective, I sat in the Nissan and watched their two-family house on Laconia. It was painted in a dull sky blue, with a dreadfully dirty white trim. The house was set inside of a wire fence with a few nuisance trees along the sides. Even now in the springtime, the plants and flowers had assumed no life out in front. Instead, weeds grew wild at the foot of the fences and in the cracks of the walkway. Dog shit had been dropped in a few places where the grass hadn't died off, and the outdoor light fixture was broken above the entrance.

It wasn't much to look at for so many hours at a time, but I had an FM radio in the car and alternated between WBLS, Power 105 and Hot 97. I also had a copy of the *Post* where they did another story about me.

THE PINK HEART MURDERER:
A HOME RUN HITTER?

*By Wilbert Matthews*

New York City, Tuesday. The killer has struck again. Yesterday morning an unidentified male Hispanic, approximately 29 years of age, was found dead on the campus of Lehman College. The victim had been dead for hours when a student found him this morning, apparently the thirtieth victim of the Pink Heart Murderer. He was tied to a tree and live rats had been stuffed down his throat, after which the victim's mouth had been taped closed. An autopsy is currently being conducted. An empty five-pound package of sugar was found next to the body. Traces of sugar were also found in and around the victim's mouth.

An officer on the scene said, "We won't know for sure until we get the coroner's report, but we suspect that since he was tied to a tree, he may have experienced some internal injuries."

Officials have asked for anyone who may have seen any suspicious activity on the Lehman College campus Monday night into early Tuesday morning to call 577-TIPS. Campus officials are also investigating; however, they were not available for comment as of press time.

"It's obvious who did this," added the officer on the scene. "There's that lipstick heart—the signature—on the victim's forehead. It doesn't take a rocket scientist to know who committed this murder. The question is, what is the killer's name and how do we find him or her? This is a sick criminal mind we're dealing with here, and he or she must be stopped." *(More about the Pink Heart murders on page 3 of the Metro News section).*

I've decided to quit my office job since the men I slay were beginning to pay so well. The dude I fed rats and sugar to had $400 in his wallet. Plus there was a gold Visa and a platinum MasterCard. I'd be careful with the credit cards, but there's no question that I'd be using them.

And remember Nicky? He was the fool I fed to the lions at the Bronx Zoo. Well, he hooked me up real nice. Mister Universal Record Deal had $500 on him. Not to mention a Rolex in his pocket. The wristband was busted, but I was still able to pawn it for $1,800.

There were other prize winnings, but nothing more than $200 in cash. Still, this was turning out to be a job that I liked and that also, coincidentally, paid well. It just so happened that the men I chose had at least a little bit of money for me to confiscate.

I was still casing the wife-beater, Freddie, and I was almost certain sure that his would be a different story. In other words, no money for River. I understood he had poor, battered Nancy to take care of, not to mention their love child. I thought about that, the child who would be left fatherless after I did what I had to do. But then, better to get rid of the asshole before he hurt the baby, too. Call it a community service I'm doing.

"HEY, SIR? SIR, could you help me out?"

"I gave at the office. Get away from my house." Freddie had just come home from work, and I was parked close enough for long enough to see Nancy go for a walk with the baby in a stroller. This was as good a time as any.

"Sir, I just need a moment of your time. Surely a man of your resources would know how to get my car started again."

"What's wrong with your car? Dead battery?"

"The battery's okay," I said, gesturing toward the Nissan. But I was thinking, it's you that's dead. "It's just . . . well . . . it's a new battery. Just got it the other day. Except, I don't think the man put the wires

on the terminals correctly. I think it's something
simple, if you'd just give me a moment, I sure
would be grateful." There I was, pouring on the
whole Pollyana routine. They fall for it ever' time.
Sucker.

"You alone? You live around here?" Freddie
asked. Now he was interested.

"Not far. Over on Eastchester, actually. But you
know . . . a single woman could get in a lot of trouble out here . . . all alone."

Freddie looked up and down the block, as
though to see if people were looking. He even
looked back at his house, maybe to see if Nancy
was looking. "Well . . . a few minutes can't hurt.
What's a pretty thing like you doin' out this way
anyhow?"

I reached in driver's side window once we
stepped up to the car and the hood popped open as
if by magic. "The truth is, I was bored at home all
alone. I just decided to go for a drive. Real tense,
ya know? I don't know what it is—just the stress of
being single, I guess." I couldn't have sent a more
direct message. I just hoped he wasn't stupid as he
looked, and that he'd catch on.

"This is a new battery?" Freddie asked. I came
around to look.

"Well . . . the man said it was new. I never really
looked, to tell the truth."

"I think he beat you, miss. Where . . . who did
your work?" Freddie had his hands on his hips now.

"Just up the block. Boston Road and Pearsal."

"Jethro? Jethro was who you went to?"

I nodded hesitantly, pretending to be the fool. Then he said, "Try it now."

I sat in the driver's seat and turned the key. The car immediately started up. "Oh my God! Thank you! You are so wonderful," I said with my brightest eyes and smile.

"You really should go back to Jethro and give him a piece of your mind. He sold you a used battery. He beat you."

"No. I'm used to some of these mechanics taking me to the cleaners. I never have been one to know what I'm talking about when it comes to cars."

"This isn't cars, miss. It's common sense. He sold you something used when it was suppose to be new."

I put on my face of shame. "I wish I had a strong, wise man to speak up for me. That's a man I'd bend over backward for. A woman's gotta have a good man in her life these days. Or else . . . this is what happens." I dropped my head and asked, "Can I pay you something for your help?"

Freddie didn't answer. He instead looked at his watch. I was sure I caught him sneaking a peek at my open shirt as well.

"Wha—? What are you doing?" I asked as he opened the car door.

"Get in. Drive me to Jethro's. You're getting a new battery right now."

"But . . . I . . . I can't drive with a perfect stranger. You might be a mad rapist or somethin'."

"Miss, this is my house over there. I just fixed your car. Now do I look like a rapist?"

"I guess not. Can I trust you?"

Freddie made a strange face. "Would you drive?"

I put the car in gear and drove slowly down the street. "What's your name anyway?"

"Freddie. And yours?"

"Catrina. Catrina Brown."

"Well, good to meet you, Catrina Brown. You can't let men take advantage of you like this."

"I know, I know. That's why I'm single right now, because my first love did me dirty."

"Your first love?"

"Yes. We went to high school together—"

"But you're what, twenty something?"

"Twenty-one. My birthday was the other day."

"So, what . . . you were with the guy for five years or so?"

"Only two. I've been single for three years now. A girl can't just give her milk away to anyone."

Freddie's response was just what I wanted. I was sure of his disbelief, to the point I could read his mind: Single for three years?!

"But I haven't been lucky enough to find a man who can really be what I need. And if he is, he's usually taken, married or gay."

Freddie made a face.

"Are you any of those?" I asked.

"Any of what?"

"Taken, married or gay," I repeated.

Freddie chuckled a bit, then he said, "No." Only he didn't face me when he said it. Freddie, the liar.

We were close to Jethro's now. Instead of driving up to the establishment, I parked across the street. I had to think quickly. Play this by ear.

"Freddie? Would you mind waiting here while I go see if he's in?"

"Of course he is. The door is usually pulled down at six, but he's always in there, still working."

"I'm sure," I said. And I put my hand on his thigh. "But let me check anyway, please?"

Freddie grinned. His eyes shot down at my hand. Then I said, "Thank you," and I caressed his cheek with the same hand. By now this scum had to have had an erection growing.

Ass wagging in my short skirt, I crossed the street and pushed my way into Jethro's. I had been looking for an opportunity to do Jethro for a long time. He was one of those weasels who took women transmission, but gave me a price break after I gave him a marathon blow job. And now, as I had promised, I was back for more.

"Oh-h-ho . . . Miss Catrina! Good to see you again. Problem with the car?"

I bit my lower lip and made bedroom eyes at Jethro. He had just rolled out from under a Pontiac and was greasy, with a yellow-toothed smile that turned my stomach.

"No. No problem with the car. Are you alone?"

He wiped his hands on an already grimy rag. "Sure am. Did you have, uhh, something in mind?"

I smiled and looked unsure of myself. Then I approached him. "Can we, ahh, go to your office again?"

"But . . . I'm kinda dirty."

"That's okay, Jethro. I think that would only make things more exciting." As I said this I was running my forefinger down his dingy coveralls, fiddling with the zipper. He shuddered, lost for words. I helped his decision-making by leading the way to the office. I played with my blouse, pretending to undo it as I switched my ass for his entertainment. I could feel him behind me, probably with his mouth watering.

Inside his small office, I closed the door and put my purse on his desk. "You mind if I unzip you, Jethro?"

"N-no, go right ahead."

I tugged slowly at the man's zipper, easing it southward. "Ooh . . . it is kinda dirty. Would you mind taking it off?"

"Oh, you bet." Jethro's voice squeaked and he rushed to get the outfit off.

In the meantime, I went to my purse and pulled out Sally. She hadn't done much work in a while thanks to my other types of "creative killings." I turned to find Jethro lifting his leg out of the overalls, now standing in socks, boxers and a T-shirt.

The boxers had tiny sunflowers printed on them. Oh brother.

With the gun behind my back, I gave Jethro a long, sultry viewing. "All ready?" I asked.

"Couldn't be any more ready, babe. Let's have it."

"You think you can let me swallow this time, instead of shootin' all over my face?"

"Sure. Why not?"

I went down on my knees and with one hand I teased Jethro, fondling his dick and balls through the opening of his boxers. "You don't mind if I pull these babies down, do you?"

"Do ya thing, baby. Work it." Jethro had a lot more confidence now, with me on my knees and all. Huh. Men and their power talk.

I pulled down his boxers, immediately smelling a day's worth of sweat and musk. I ignored the awful, sour smell and stroked what was now a full erection. "Jethro, how about turning around for me. Let me get a little adventurous, do you mind?" He was jubilant.

"Oh no, baby. I don't mind whatsoever!" Jethro did as I asked, turning around and placing his hands on a cabinet filled with his mechanic's tools.

"Jethro?"

"Yes, mama?"

"You feel this?"

"Oh, I sure do, Miss Catrina. What is it? It's kinda cold."

"I don't think you'll wanna move, Jethro. See,

this cold steel here"—I added some pressure, the tip of the gun now at the weasel mechanic's asshole—"this is a .38 caliber Smith and Wesson. She's one of my best friends, actually. So say hi to Sally."

Jethro was stunned, standing there as if a policeman were behind him about to do a pat down. "Say 'Hi, Sally.'" I encouraged Jethro's response with a bit more pressure from the nose of my weapon.

Jethro stuttered, but he managed to say, "H-hi, Sally."

"Good. That's real good," Then I backed away, humored at the sight of this man standing in his T-shirt with his boxers pulled down to his ankles. I didn't really want to shoot Jethro in his ass, it was just the threat I wanted to make clear. And besides, Freddie would be in to check on me any minute now. So Jethro was an important part of my plan.

"Miss? Hello? Jethro? Anyone here?"

"In here, Freddie! Help!!" I uttered my distress and stood back in a combat firing stance, with my arms and Sally fully extended.

"Catrina? Jethro? What's going on in here? What's taking so long—?" Freddie lost his voice once he realized what was going on. Jethro's naked ass was the first thing to catch his eye. Next was me and my gun.

"Whoa . . . what the fuck? You ain't gotta shoot the dude?" A note of surprise was in Freddie's voice.

"Freddie, our friend Jethro needs some attention. Why don't you help him out?" I gestured with the .38. But it only made poor Freddie confused.

"Attention? What kind of attention do he need from me?"

"The type of attention he usually gets from the women he cheats out of their hard-earned money." To Jethro, I said, "Isn't that right?" Jethro didn't respond, so I squeezed off one round into the glass tool cabinet there in front of him. Both men jerked as if I'd shot *them*. I made my point, that this wasn't a game.

"I said, isn't that *right*!?"

"Yes, yes, yes, ohhh yes!" Jethro cried out, visibly shaking.

"What's this gotta do with me?" Freddie demanded.

"Everything." I scowled. "This has everything to do with you. You're a menace to women, to your wife, to your child—"

"But I'm . . . I'm not married. You talkin' to the wrong person." Freddie's arms were raised in protest.

"Nancy Grimes. Does that name ring a bell? You're a menace to Nancy, yo' baby momma."

"Did she put you up to this?" Freddie asked. Except he asked in such a way, with his hands on his hips and his angry lizard eyes, that I was reminded of the monster he was inside. It only helped to motivate me. To get this over with.

"Shut up! And get over there by Jethro—right now!" I could've chewed my words as tightly as my teeth clenched together.

Finally, Freddie was close enough to Jethro.

"Spank him, Freddie. Spank him hard and tell him how cruel he's been to the women he stole from. Do it!" Freddie gave me a crazy look, but mine was much crazier. Plus, I had Sally pointed right at his head. You can't argue with Sally.

The first smack was dull and uneventful. I could see that Freddie wasn't into this like I wanted.

"Harder! And I wanna hear you tell him what I said. Do it Freddie, or else I blow a hole right through your ass."

Freddie spanked Jethro harder. The smacking sound filled the room, even making me twitch down between my legs.

"Jethro, you're an asshole for taking women's money . . . you're a goddamn jerk . . . a fucking . . . fool . . ."

"Harder, Freddie!" I said, thoroughly enjoying the look on Jethro's face. He was bracing himself, anticipating each whack before it hit him.

This went on for a few minutes, with Freddie now turning both of Jethro's ass cheeks red and sore.

"Hello?" A female voice came through the office door seconds before she did. "Jethro?" the woman inquired. She was about five feet, six inches tall, rail-thin but with perky breasts and ass. She was pretty in the face with a peanut-butter complexion, only she had so much makeup on. Plus her hair was wiry, the results of a long day's work.

"Might as well come in and enjoy the show, sweetie," I said. I used my foot to push an office chair over to her. Without really pointing the gun at her, I urged her to sit. She did.

"What's happening?" She asked this with an expression of marvel mixed with fear. She was so damned pretty, too. I hated the thoughts on my mind . . . what I'd have to do to her now that she was in the way.

Jethro said, "Please, miss—don't let my customers see me like this. Please."

"Shut up, Jethro. That's the least of your worries," I said, adding to the lady, "What's your name, miss?"

"Mavis," the woman answered in a fragile tone.

"And what did you come to Jethro for, a fix-up?" I said this to both her and Jethro, letting them both know that I was on to the game. The favors Jethro demanded in exchange for money owed.

"Uh . . . yeah. Something like that," she answered.

"Tell me the truth, Mavis. How much do you owe Jethro here? And don't make me ask you twice."

"Two thousand. I had engine trouble."

"Mmm-hmm, is that so? And tell me, is your car here? Is he holding it hostage while he's, ahh, working on it?"

"I guess . . ."

"You guess? That's a yes or no question, Mavis."

"Yes," she responded, turning her eyes down and away from the Freddie-Jethro activity.

"Oh, it's okay, doll. You can watch. There's a whole lot more show to come," I said. And then I heard a giggle.

Shit.

There was another woman, a short Latina it looked like, with a shapely petite body, long brown hair and big beautiful eyes. She was just outside the office in the dark.

"Excuse me," I said. "You need to come in and join the party."

"I'm—oh my God. I'm sorry. I must have the wrong garage."

"Ohhh, no you don't," I said. And I made sure she saw Sally. "Come on in—might as well. Don't be afraid, just have a seat next to Mavis here." I made another chair available. It had ripped upholstery, but it would do. "What's your name, girlfriend?"

"Bonnie."

"Mavis, meet Bonnie. Bonnie, Mavis. Wow, who knew you two were gonna have such a devoted audience? Mmm, and lemme guess: she's another happy customer, huh, Jethro? Huh? Give it to him, Freddie! He's runnin' a goddamned whorehouse!"

Bonnie couldn't help her chuckle. And now Mavis was beginning to laugh, too.

"How about it, ladies? How 'bout we see a real show?" I licked my lips and found a desk to perch my ass on. "How about it, Mavis? Would you like to see Jethro go down on Freddie here?"

Mavis made a face. This was obviously something that embarrassed her.

"How about you, Bonnie? Wanna see Jethro suck Freddie's dick?"

Bonnie put her hand over her mouth. Her eyes glistened with excitement. Apparently, she was getting as much thrill out of this as I was.

"Jethro? Do the honors. And Freddie? I'm gonna tell you this one time and one time only, whip the motherfucker out. Jethro? You can get on your knees and start suckin'. And suck it good . . . just like you gettin' it sucked by your customers, go on and give it to Freddie."

We watched as the two sideshow freaks got into position. Freddie was fuming and I know he was hoping I'd loosen my grip on the gun or maybe take my eyes off him enough for him to make a move. But I was as sharp as a tack right now. Nothing was gonna ruin this moment.

Jethro was on his knees now. He hesitated.

"Maybe you need encouragement, Jethro?" I stepped around and held the nose of the gun a foot or two from his calf. "I'll make it so you'll be limping the rest of your life."

Jethro shivered and wagged his head. His hand went up to grip Freddie's penis and, just like a first

timer, he took an inch or so of it in his mouth. Jethro
wasn't fooling me, though. I could tell that this was
smoke and mirrors, with only his lips touching, hiding the fact that his tongue and cheeks were in no
way in on this endeavor.

"Jethro? Suck that dick, man! I wanna hear your
tongue and gums slurpin' like his dick is a fuckin'
buttered crab leg!" My small audience giggled,
somehow oblivious to the threat of the gun in my
hand. But both Jethro and Freddie knew the sound
of Sally's voice. They knew I meant business.

Jethro got to sucking and I made sure to study
Freddie's face, how difficult it was for him to handle the sensation of the blow job, the discomfort of
three onlookers and the confusion in his own
mind—another man sucking his dick? The effect
of it all, the two men and the two women, also took
a toll on me. What would I do now? Kill everybody? It would be a first, and I knew I could follow
through.

Except these two women were harmless and, like
me, they had been taken advantage of. And Jethro?
Sure, he conned women into sex and took their
money, but was it worth the unique brand of death I
dished? And then there was Freddie. Oh yes, he de-
served it twice over. But the witnesses! Oh No!

"Stop, stop, stop," I told Jethro. "Freddie's enjoying this too much. Freddie? On your hands and
knees. Now. Jethro? You done good. But now I want
you to stick it in Freddie's ass—" "Oh, shit-no. The

fuck he will!" Freddie argued and got back up to his feet. In that split second I stepped over and shot Freddie in the lower leg. He fell over in extreme pain. A gasp and scream came from Bonnie and Mavis as I got out of Freddie's way, turning Sally on Jethro so he wouldn't try anything.

"See, girls, this isn't so funny after all. Our lives are at stake here. Yours and mine. See, Freddie here likes to beat up women. I mean, he beats the shit out of 'em. Probably rapes 'em, too. I can't for sure confirm that since I'm not with him twenty-four seven, but if you do it to one . . ."

I was trying to sell this thing as best I could, but Mavis was in tears, afraid for her life. This compli-cated things. If I could only be sure of these two women, I wouldn't have to worry about the police and jail . . . and if I was tied to all the other killings, there was death row to consider.

Bonnie hugged Mavis in some sign of sisterly affection as she and I locked eyes. I could see that Bonnie wasn't afraid of me. It was like she could read my mind. Somewhere in her big beautiful eyes I saw an ally . . . a comrade. I turned my at-tention back to Freddie, who was crying in an-guish, blood soaking his pants.

"Now, Freddie, I'm gonna make this simple. You do what the fuck I tell you, and you might live to see tomorrow. You don't, I'm gonna have to help take you out of your misery." I stuck the gun to Freddie's head.

That was when Jethro made his move. He dove at me, catching me off-guard. I fell over Freddie with Jethro scrambling on top of both of us. Sally went flying across the office floor while I fought and scratched to get out from under the mechanic. But now Freddie was helping him, too. Both of them punched and grabbed at me. I felt pain in my thighs and ribs, but things were happening so damned fast that it was all one brief outburst of roughhousing.

I was fighting for much more than immediate freedom; much more was at stake than the challenge Jethro and Freddie had for me. I felt like I was fighting the world. I eventually got to sink my teeth into someone's wrist and there was a holler. I also got a kick in from my position on the floor. A grunt sounded.

Then there was a gunshot. It was warning enough for all of us to freeze, wondering who'd been hit . . . wondering who pulled the trigger.

"Get off of her!" a voice shouted. Then I realized it was Bonnie, with the smoking gun in hand. "Jethro, raise up 'fore I pop a cap in you."

I winced as I got to my feet, some kind of pain along my side. Jethro also got up, but Freddie was still there on the floor with nothing but thoughts and rage to nurse his gunshot wound I'd given him. There was a suspension in time just then. What now? Police? Handcuffs? The evening news?

"Okay, Bonnie . . . lemme have that gun. You

did good." Jethro was pulling up his boxers now, about to approach the Latina.

In a brief glance, I saw that there was skin and blood under my nails. Whoever had experienced my claws was unimportant just now.

"Stay right there, Jethro," Bonnie said, holding Sally out to me butt-first.

"What are you— Hey! Don't give her that! Bonnie!"

"Miss . . . whoever you are, I hope this doesn't mean you'll be shooting all of us," Bonnie added.

I took the gun cautiously. I did have a comrade! "Thank you, baby. You're making the right decision."

"God-*damn!* You dumb bitch! Now look what you went and did."

"Fuck you, Jethro. She's right. You ain't doin' us right. My sister said you beat her out of six hundred, plus you been forcin' me to suck your goddamn dick—fuck you and die, bastard. I hope she makes Swiss cheese outta you!"

I smiled from ear to ear, hoping Mavis got something out of this.

"Now that I think of it," added Bonnie, "didn't the lady say she wanted you to stick the man in his butt?"

I coulda laughed when I heard that. Was this my new partner? Bonnie and Bonnie? Gun in hand, I said, "Freddie? You heard the woman. Let's go on with the show. Hands and knees! Right now!" As

Freddie whimpered and got into position, I suddenly realized how this would play out. I didn't have to kill people after all. I'd just make homosexuals out of 'em and go about my business. It would be just revenge for Bonnie and Mavis to watch, and the two would-be men would have to live with this for the rest of their lives. They wouldn't share what happened here in Jethro's office with the police, the press or anyone else for that matter. Who would?

Mavis and Bonnie and I had ourselves some tremendous laughs as Jethro pounded his stuff into Freddie's ass. Oh God, the faces that Freddie made! God! I know I experienced a climax somewhere between Freddie being fucked and then Jethro being sucked. Jethro had a Polaroid camera on a shelf in his office, too. Probably for those insurance fraud jobs he does. I had Mavis take some pictures for all of us. I got a few myself. Then I told Freddie and Jethro that if word of this ever got out that I'd make so many reprints of the snapshots that the two would be made into poster boys for the next "Just Say No" campaign.

THAT NIGHT I told Brandon, my golden retriever, about the festivities at Jethro's Auto Shop as we cuddled on my bed to watch our usual hour of Tom and Jerry cartoons. Brandon didn't seem too interested, all focused on the cat and mouse duo like they were the world's greatest entertainers. But I was still in my glory, reliving the images in my mind. It was more fulfilling than all the blood I spilled, all the bodies I maimed and all the havoc I brought into so many men's lives.

I couldn't help but play with myself as I lay there naked beside Brandon. Usually, Brandon would smell my juices when I dipped my fingers in and out of my pussy and either snuggle up and lick at my breasts or, better, go downtown and make a meal out of me. But not if Tom and Jerry was on. It made me crazy to think that my dog put a cartoon before some good sex with Mama River.

# SISSY

"I'M GLAD YOU were able to make it, Officer Dickerson,"

"It was a direct order, sir. If you remember, you said to report to your office at twenty-one-hundred hours. You didn't say *please join me.*"

"Yeah, yeah, you're right. I suppose it was an order. Have a seat, Dickerson."

*Another order? I guess it's official this time.*

"Is something wrong, sir?" When I looked at Sergeant Meadows I was always reminded of Porky Pig from the Warner Brothers cartoons.

I hate to always make a cartoon out of things, but he did actually resemble the pig. Just like Maritza talked like squeaky Olive Oyl. God bless 'em, but some of the men on the force kind of resemble cartoon characters also. Williams had big balloon arms like Popeye. Tomanelli looks like George Jetson. Rosario is huge, with jet black hair and beady

eyes. He reminds me of Space Ghost. Captain
Bartholemew is short with rough facial features—
pock marks, scars and all. So I can't help but picture Yosemite Sam when I see that short runt of a
man. There are twin brothers at the precinct; both
have unibrows and crew cuts that shoot out into an
arrow at the forehead. So the Sullivan brothers per-
sonify Heckle and Jeckle, the magpies.

It's not an obsession I have with cartoons, it's
just that I've been seeing a lot of old ones lately.
The Cartoon Network has to be one of April's favorite channels, considering how it's always on
when I come home. Sometimes I think she looks at
it as an escape of some kind; a step away from all
the religious business, where sins are sort of permitted.

As far as I'm concerned, the woman needs a
dose of reality. I might do as she asks; I might go
ahead and allow her to come along for a ride in the
squad car one of these days. Of course Maritza
would have to approve because the commanding
officer wouldn't. That means we would be going
against orders.

"Is something wrong. Hmmm . . . well, I suppose it depends on how you look at things, Officer
Dickerson. Do you remember our little, ahh, encounter at the 77th? What was that, two and a half
years ago?"

"I try not to, sir. You did say that I should wipe
that from my mind . . . that it never happened."

"Yeah, I know what I said, but some things change, know what I mean?"

"No. I don't."

"Oh, a little arrogant, are we?" Sergeant Meadows took a folder out of his desk. "I have a report here regarding the incident at Gun Hill Road. The scuffle at the used car lot. Does that ring a bell?"

"Yes. I remember it well."

"Very well then. At least we're on the same page. Now, as the officer in charge of Internal Affairs in Brooklyn, I did you a favor some time ago, did I not?"

"Y-yes. You did. For a price."

He chuckled. "Never mind the cost. Point is, I got you out of a tough situation. Got you transferred just like that." He snapped his fingers. "And now trouble is beginning to brew over here."

"Trouble? Wha—?"

"Now, now. We need to watch our tone of voice, Officer. The report I received earlier this week says you allowed a Nancy Grimes to attack your partner, Garcia, while she was securing a suspect in an arrest for assault."

"Yeah, but she was the victim, and—"

"Please. You'll have an opportunity to answer the charges," he announced with an air of ultimate authority.

"Charges?!"

"Exactly. I didn't read you your rights or invite a witness into these proceedings because I knew that we'd be able to, well, work things out. If you know what I mean." Meadows flashed that cunning smile at me. He could have just as well said it out loud: I have the upper hand. There is no way out of this.

Thing is, I wasn't going for it. This was bullshit. And I stood up to tell him just that.

"You know what, Sergeant? I do know exactly what you mean . . ." I approached the front of his desk. "And from now on? If these so-called charges should come up again, and if I'm ordered to report to I.A.B. again, then make sure it's during respectable hours so I can have my lawyer with me!" I slammed his door when I left.

"Bastard," I growled as I stormed out of the precinct. It was only 9:30 in the evening, and for some reason I was sick to my stomach. I was at the back of the station house when I spit up my dinner on the nearest parked vehicle. When it was all over, I had to laugh. The irony! What were the odds that I'd get an upset stomach and that I'd let it all out just as I passed Sergeant Meadows' car?

Usually I'd have caught a ride with Maritza, but I decided I needed the fresh air, so I took a walk up to White Plains Road and ended up having a drink at the Lucky Love Lounge.

"Sex on the Beach, please."

"You okay, baby?" asked the bartender. She had a slightly freckled, wheat-brown complexion and wore her hair in a short bob. Her clothes were fitted as well; she was probably real proud of those tits and that ass.

"I'm good. Just a long day." I sighed. "A long, frustrating day."

"You're five-oh, aren't you?" It was more an answer than a question.

"Yep. You called it. Head to toe, that's me. New York's finest." I said this with some overexaggeration as the woman poured my drink.

"Oh I'm not mad at you, girlfriend. I'm proud of you, if anything. I'm sure you're pullin' a heavy load . . . oh no, don't bother. This one's on the house."

"No, baby. I don't roll that way. I pay my way."

"Sorry, girl. Everybody pays their way around here, cops included. But this time? For you? I'm pickin up the tab," said the bartender. And she pushed my hand away and cut her eyes at me. I wasn't up to arguing. Not tonight.

"Okay, what's the deal? You got problems here? Somebody shakin' your place down? It must be somethin'—some kinda favor you need?"

"Can't a girl just make a kind gesture? Jeez."

I took a swallow of the liquor. "Sorry. It's just that . . . well, in my field we have to assume that there's a reason behind everything. Everybody's a liar . . . or they want something," I said.

"Wow. What a turnoff. And you have to live like this every day?"

"Goes with the job. Lies. Hustlers, con artists, thieves . . . all of 'em trying to get over somehow, someway. Either that, or I'm a sounding board for people to bounce their frustrations off of. People. I swear . . . they just wanna be heard. Thing is, that's what 911 has become. But the number should be 1-800-listen to me, or 1-900-solve my big ole problem."

The bartender laughed. "You're so funny! I swear, your job is just about the same as mine. I have to be the good listener every shift. It takes so much patience sometimes. I feel like a therapist."

"You too, huh?"

"Mmm-hmm . . . but most times, especially with the guys who come through, it's a big ole confidence game to try and get me into bed."

"Well, shit, I don't have that problem. In fact, that sounds like a good problem. Like, you can take your pick, can't you?"

"I guess. But you know, AIDS is out here, girl. I can't just sleep around with anybody, like they could in the good ole days . . ." Somewhere between the bartender's "good ole days" comment and sunrise, I ended up all buzzed from three or four drinks, naked from head to toe, with my head between this woman's legs. They said there's a first time for everything, but somehow all of the nervousness or first-time jitters that I might have experienced in such a situation didn't get in my way. I could recall only pleasure and released tensions. I felt my anxieties being abandoned and I felt liberation, all at once. I surrendered all my homophobic beliefs and submerged myself in an ocean of carnal passion. I could do anything with this woman. I knew how to pleasure her, because I knew how I wanted to be pleased myself.

In turn, she was a feisty and aggressive vixen . . . a devil, really, how she did things with her tongue and lips, making me continuously climax and collapse until my body had been vacuumed of all its senses. I was satisfied until I went numb.

When I woke up, I was in another world. The daylight made everything in this woman's home so bright and sunny. An atmosphere that might inspire ideas and hope. A new game.

"Sorry to wake you, hon, but I wasn't sure when you had to report to work."

It was six in the morning. I suddenly had this woman's face inches away from my own. And then she kissed my forehead, her hand stroking my unsheeted body.

Oh my God . . . what the fuck did I do?!

I shivered, with a new fear, wondering exactly how far this had gone. And then the flashbacks started. I remembered being wet between my legs, wetter than any man had ever made me. I remembered this woman's hands becoming familiar with my curves and my most sensitive areas. There was kissing, nibbling and licking that made me feel unreal, as if I had been twisted inside out for the want of some release. All of those incredible feelings, and yet I couldn't recall the woman's name.

"I made us eggs over easy. Just a guess. I figured everybody can deal with eggs over easy. Here's a fruit dish to start with, gotta run and see to the smoked turkey sausage." My new friend literally danced out of the bedroom; ass switching, clothed only with a "My Boyfriend Is Out of Town" T-shirt.

All this attention I was getting reminded me of so long ago when I would go out of the way to earn approval from my father. I was such a little sassy so-and-so, but I could still remember the time. Now, with a breakfast tray propped over my outstretched legs and an inviting bowl of mixed fruit in my face, I wasn't sure what this woman wanted from me. Did she want my approval? And now that I was fully awake, my mind was clear enough to make a more thorough observation of my surroundings.

The bartender lived well. Her bedroom was something out of a mafia princess handbook. Spacious, with high ceilings. A monstrous bed, a few indoor trees, a vanity fit for an actress and thick white carpet to blend in with the walls. There were just two wall hangings, artist's renditions of my bartender-friend in the nude. The poses were sensual, bordering on naughty. Sheer curtains permitted the sunlight to intrude through three large picture windows. *Who is this girl?*

Ever the policewoman, I snooped instead of eating the fruit. A silk kimono robe was draped over the back of a chair, good enough to cover myself. My first thought was to shoot into the bathroom, but I was sidetracked by the view out of the windows. We were high up—a penthouse? This was some marvelous view, overlooking many, many rooftops, with the skyline of New York City in the distance.

"Nice view, huh?"

"Wow," I growled. "Are we even in the Bronx?"

"Of course," she said as if I was out of my mind. "What'd you think, we got on a plane or something?" She put down two plates on trays which she had set up opposite the bed. She then approached me. "This is my crib, boo. We're on Westchester Avenue and you're looking south. What, you forget everything we talked about last night?"

Jesus Christ, she's hugging me! I had to put my hand against the curtains and window to brace myself. The spasm that ran through my body was enough to collapse me.

"You okay?"

"I . . . yeah." I sighed.

"This is new for you, the whole girl-girl thing, huh?"

"New is not the word."

"Well, if it's any consolation, I'm kind of shocked, too. I told you, this was a first for me."

"You did?"

"Mmm-hmm. Last night."

"Last night, last night, what the hell happened

last night? I had two drinks and all of a sudden I'm knee-deep in a pussy-eating party?"

"Depends on who was doing the eating. And you had more than two drinks, girlfriend. It was more like four," she added.

"Oh that would do it."

"And you should know that you were the one who asked me out. To put it in your own words, you said, 'I would give my left tit to fuck you tonight.'"

"Whoa! I said that?"

"Yes, you did. And chile, I heard all the lines there are to hear, and I never heard that one."

"I've been watchin' too many movies," I said, for lack of a better excuse.

"Okay . . ." She backed up a little, her hands falling away from my curves. "So does this mean that what we did was a fluke?" The signs of resentment and rejection showed in her eyes.

"I don't know what it means, to be perfectly honest. I just know this is . . . well, it's different," I admitted.

"Different, as in new? Or different, as in you feel sick?"

"I don't feel sick, I can tell you that."

"Does it at least feel good? Do you feel satisfied?"

I was hugging myself now, a little naked in my revealing so much to this perfect stranger. Maybe not so perfect after all. I exhaled and replied, "I'm fine. I think I'll survive."

"That's not what I asked you," she said, arms folded.

"Yes, okay. Is that what you wanna hear? I felt good. It feels good. I'm thoroughly satisfied. You twisted my body like a pretzel . . . yesyesyes! Are you happy? Is that what you wanna hear? Does that make you happy to know you turned me out?"

"Well, you don't have to be miserable about it," she huffed.

"Don't you get it? I feel strange. Like I've gone through an out-of-body experience. Isn't that how a normal person's supposed to feel when they've done . . . well . . . this? To tell the truth, I don't know what to feel, or what to say. I kinda wish I could just disappear for an hour or two, have some time to think things over."

"Fine."

"Don't get an attitude, this has nothing to do with you. It's just me. Shit I'm going through."

"Should I take you home? Call you a cab?"

"Oh, just sit down and eat," I said. "Before the food gets cold."

HER NAME WAS Eve. She was just about my height and looked pretty, even without makeup. She told me she grew up in Yonkers, ran away from home at age fifteen and ended up with a drug dealer who was shot down in a bust.

"So that explains all this," I said.

"All what?"

"You're living like a goddamn princess, Eve. Married to the mob."

"Don't judge a book by its cover, Sissy. I think even without my ex-boyfriend, I could've made it on my own."

"Right. And pigs fly." Eve made a face. "Listen, I'm not knocking your capabilities, girl. I just know for a fact you had a few shortcuts here and there. Not that a lavish Bronx penthouse is gonna make you the first lady, but it's something. It's a resource."

"And sucking the president's dick makes you first lady—or a mistress, anyway," said Eve. "So, I sucked dick and got my own crib and wardrobe and Porsche. What's the difference? I still put my work in. I did what I had to do to survive. And now I have a good job, so I'm doin' what I gotta do to live. Any way you slice it, I'm bustin' my ass just like the next nine-to-five girl."

I shrugged off her explanation, not clear about the distinction or association between hard work and blow jobs. To me, one would always be a lot easier than the other.

"You think we rushed things? I mean, I tend to have a gut feeling about people, so it's easy to make a decision like I did about you. Only now, I'm wondering if you think you're any different than other women because you're five-oh."

"It is different, Eve. It's a lot different. Not that

I'm better. I suppose I just have another take on things. Another perspective."

"How so? Because you carry a gun and badge?"

"Not. People always underestimate police. And they always, *always* underestimate a policewoman. You'll never know the shit I gotta deal with. You wear heels, a flimsy blouse and skirt to work. Me? I wear a Kevlar vest to keep the bullets away. What you watch on the Discovery Channel, Court TV and in the movies, I live every day. The guns, the car chases and dead bodies are real for me, Eve. And it's just not a now and then thing. It's an everyday thing.

"Whenever the sun rises, I'm just another performer on the real-life stage with the murderers, thieves and prostitutes. I'm in the orchestra pit with a band of jealous wives, violent boyfriends and the children—oh God, the children. They're abused, battered and scarred for life. They're part of the band as victims, and they're part of the audience, absorbing all of the images and patterns of their parents; and they have no choice but to accept this antisocial behavior as normal."

"Okay, Sissy. I'm feelin' all of that. But you did sign up and train for that job, didn't you?"

"Yes. And? Because I trained for the job doesn't prevent the effect it's had on me. I look at people different nowadays. A kid on the street to me today is much different than three years ago. Instead of a

playful, innocent youth, I see a potential gun-
toting bully who maybe just experimented with
putting a cat in a microwave. I don't see the average little ole lady as harmless and docile, but as a
stubborn, psychotic bitch who carries a six-inch
blade or a loaded .357, ready to slay the next person who knocks at her door claiming to be a salesman. Or as a nut who dials 911, complaining that
her next-door neighbor is a devil worshipper, or
worse—an alien who can see through walls.

"And then there are the men; they're no longer
hardworking do-gooders. They're gang members,
pimps, johns, rapists, drug dealers, con artists and
pedophiles—and if they're not today, then they
just might be tomorrow. I'm fucked up, Eve. I'm
numb and jaded. I don't have faith anymore. I
don't have hope. I don't even think I can love
again. I used to think that wearing a uniform would
make me a hero or at least a role model. Maybe I
could find a good man. But all I am is a target. A
moderator, a therapist and a target."

After I spilled my stress and frustrations, Eve
apologized for underestimating me. Then we made
love again. This time, it was her doing most of the
work—deep sea diving, she called it. I would've
called in and asked for the day off, but the chief
would only ask if I was crazy, and he'd holler
about being understaffed. So I was in the strange
predicament of having to wear some of Eve's
undergarments—her bra size was close enough to

mine—and I put back on my uniform. Lucky for me yesterday's vomit washed off real easy.

Eve drove me to the station in time to make the 8 A.M. roll call and I had to ask her to refrain from kissing me good-bye.

"You weren't embarrassed last night . . . or this morning when I ate your pussy," Eve said with an attitude.

"Don't start with me, girl," I said. And I hopped out of the car hoping that no fellow officer noticed me in this flaming red Porsche.

"I'll call you."

"Yeah. I think I heard that before," Eve shot back. Then she threw the car in gear and peeled out, back tires smoking.

Funny thing was, I actually meant what I said.


**MARITZA PULLED ME** to the side before roll call began. "Did you hear? They found another body last night. They say was another one of ours."

"Ours?"

"Yes, Sissy. Another of our domestic disputes. Remember, the guy from the used car lot? The one with the girlfriend, Nancy Grimes?"

"Oh, shit. The lady who jumped you? Sergeant Meadows from I.A.B. called me on that yesterday. Said he was considering charges."

"Sissy, I promise you I had nothing to do with that. There were the police reports—but you know we have to file those."

"I'm not trippin,' Garcia. The man's an asshole. Tell me about . . ." I tried to recall his name. There were so many whom we dealt with from day to day.

"Freddie Cox," Maritza completed my thought.

"Huh?"

"His name. Freddie Cox. They found him hanging out of a second-floor window over on Laconia. Tied a rope to a radiator and jumped out of the window. Suicide. No letter, no nothin'."

"Damn," I said, with little change in my expression.

Then Maritza said, "If only every wife beater could do that, it'd save us a lotta paperwork."

I smirked and wagged my head.

"You're brutal, Garcia."

"But I didn't tell you the half of it. Homicide is adding this to the list of the Pink Heart murders. They think there's a link."

"Oh? From a suicide? What, did the killer push Cox out of the window?"

"Nothin' like that. More like this makes fifteen out of thirty that have ties to domestic calls. *Our* domestic calls."

*"Roll call!"*

"Get ready for another visit from Homicide," Maritza said. "You know how these guys are, pullin' at any strings they can get their hands on—especially since the killer's got them on a ghost hunt."

I shrugged off the mention and joined Maritza among the four dozen other officers. The cattle call.

As close as the Pink Heart Murderer was to our tour of duty, it really wasn't our department. So all I could do was shrug. My days as a rookie were behind me; stolen bicycles, petty larceny, shoplifting and traffic stops were not our job, even if we still had to be alert for such things. Domestic squabbles, fights and arrests was workload enough for two shifts, much less the eight-to-four tour. As long as this murderer or murderess doesn't come within the reach of my Glock 9; then Homicide would have their work cut out for them.

"REMEMBER A FEW months ago? You were telling me about one of your officer buddies who walked into an armed robbery at a bodega?"

"It's been a long day, April, and I'm hankerin for a shower and my pillow."

"Hankerin'? Where'd that word come from?"

"You. I read your *Today's Black Woman* article. Something about a new female recording artist who you said was hungry for a Soul Train Award."

April came up with a belly laugh.

"But bear with me for a sec, Sissy. I think I can help you with some of your stress."

"You? You can help me? With some of my stress? Oh, gee . . . I really need to hear this one," I said.

"Okay, hear me out. The bodega cop—"

"Tomanelli. Looks like George Jetson."

"Okay. So, George Jetson foils the bodega hold-up . . ."

Foils? This woman is hilarious!

"Next thing you know, he gets some kind of award from the mayor of New York; then comes the raise, and now he's doin' what?"

"Special Investigations."

"Right. I remember you told me about that. You were pissed off because you said he had a rabbi— one of them angels that can make things happen for a cop."

"All right. I'm with you so far. But how's this gonna help relieve my stress, April?"

"Dig it, Sissy. If I help you solve this Pink Heart Murderer bit, you'll not only get a raise or an award, but you'll probably have everybody at the 52nd kissin' your . . . feet."

I laughed when April said that, because for a minute I swore she was gonna say ass. Miss Bible Study makes a jackmove. "So what do you think?"

I forked up my last bite of the chicken Caesar salad and took a second or two to chew and swallow. "Actually? I like it. But April? I'm goin' to bed. We'll kick it tomorrow. Sunday's my day off, so I don't mind discussin' things Saturday night." I wiped my mouth and got up to leave the table. "By the way," I added. "Could you do me a favor and a half?"

"What's that?" asked April, happy about the prospects of us becoming a team.

"Could you feed Coco Puff for me? Otherwise that bitch is gonna keep me awake."

April nodded and grimaced at the same time. Yes, she would take care of my dog, but no, I didn't have to go and use that word.

I've noticed a big change in April since she moved in. She seems a lot more confident, content in many ways, and I'm not 100 percent sure, but I believe my live-in, born-agin Christian is getting some dick in a big way. Sooner or later she'll have to tell me the down-low, before I get to snoopin'. And I guess she'd eventually find out about Eve and me. Already I could hear April's response. "Blasphemous!"

I've been seeing Eve for weeks, and the two of us have explored each other in every way imaginable. I honestly didn't know that two women could find so many positions, so many creative ways to get off. I can honestly say that, since being involved with Eve, I haven't thought about a man at all. I wondered if this meant I was now officially a lesbian. No matter. As long as I was happy. And indeed, Eve was making me extremely happy.

IT WAS ON a Sunday morning that someone knocked at my apartment door. I moaned and rolled out of bed, realizing that April was off to church and that the door obviously wasn't gonna answer itself. I smacked Coco Puff's ass and she followed.

"Who?" I said. Coco Puff barked once, her way of echoing me.

"It's Sergeant Meadows, open up. I need to talk to you."

I pulled Coco Puff into April's room and shut the door. "It better be important, Meadows," I said as I unhooked the chain and undid the locks. I pulled open the door and added, "If not, I'm gonna be the one bringing charges."

"Save the bullshit, Dickerson. We got business to talk about." Meadows pushed past me with his leather briefcase in hand.

On Sunday morning?

I shut the door and folded my arms. I still had on my robe and my hair was a screamin' mess. "Okay, what?"

Meadows was seated on the couch with the devil's eye. "I think you'd better change your tone with me, Sissy. You're in no position to get nasty."

"What do you expect? It's goddamned Sunday morning. Do the paperboys even get up this early?"

"Sit down, Sissy."

Sissy again? This must be good.

"I said sit," he commanded.

My arms folded still, I made a face and sat in the love seat across from the couch. The glass coffee table was the only thing to separate us. And the way he was looking at me made me feel naked. "I'm sitting. Now what's this about?"

Meadows pulled three photos out of his briefcase and tossed them on the table. The photos were black-and-white and the subject was a woman in a trench coat. "You recognize this woman?"

I picked up the photos and reviewed them. I shrugged and dropped them back on the table. "Should I?"

"No clue, huh? Okay, well, let me fill you in on some details. First of all, I grabbed these photos and their negatives out of a folder belonging to Homicide. Of course you know they're investigating the Pink Heart murders . . . yes, of course you do. Anyways, I grabbed these photos on a wild hunch, Sissy. Wanna know what my hunch was?"

My elbow on my knee and my chin in my palm, I waited for the great revelation from Porky Pig.

"Of course you wanna know. Probably already know. My hunch, Sissy, was that since more than half of the Pink Heart murders were in some way connected to your domestic calls—yours and Officer Garcia's, that is—it was possible that either Garcia or you were somehow involved. So after careful consideration, I checked the file on the investigation. And bingo. Whaddaya know? Some snapshots were taken by a building's security camera about two months ago. Of course there were a number of photos of a number of people. But considering that the word is this murderer is actually a murderess, I pulled the photos of females. Now, during the time of this particular homicide there were just two women who entered the building . . . an older woman and a younger woman."

I sat and stared at Meadows for a short time, but it felt like forever.

"I can't believe you're sitting here and accusing me of murder—Not murder. Not just one murder. Murders, plural."

"My hunch is that you, Miss Sissy Dickerson, are the femme fatale—the black widow—the god-damned Pink Heart Murderer."

"Okay, Sergeant. Are you quite done? I mean, are you through with your hunches? Because if you are, I'm on my day off. And I'm about to get back to sleep. I—"

"Sissy. I sat in my own car, across the street from your apartment building, just weeks ago. I saw this person"—Meadows picked up a photo and poked at it violently—"leave this building. I followed this person to Laconia, over behind the bowling alley, Gun Hill Lanes. Does that ring a bell? And I watched this person, I watched *you* join a man, a man now known as the late Freddie Cox, and you two drove up to Boston Road, to an auto me-chanic's establishment. Jethro's, I believe it was."

"You're dreaming, Meadows."

"I'm dreaming? My lyin' eyes, huh? And then this Cox fella winds up hangin' himself? Just days after your little trip to Jethro's? The same Cox you arrested?"

Meadows reached for the other two photos, but I got to them first. I gave them a closer look. As the seconds passed, I had a flash. I saw beyond the sunglasses the woman wore in the photo. Beyond the wig and the trench coat.

April! Oh my God! April is the killer!

I almost choked on the idea, it was so far-fetched. So crazy. It couldn't be. She wouldn't hurt a fly. She doesn't even curse! I immediately felt ambushed. Set up. Framed. Damn it. I knew April inside out. Or did I? There was just no way. I also knew Meadows. He was a slimeball. He could've been lying about any number of things. Not my born-again Christian friend!

"What're you thinking about, Dickerson? Your future? Your job? Death row?"

I said nothing, suddenly afraid and shaken. Faces and bodies were skating around in my head in slow motion. I saw all of those photos of dead men, victims whom the homicide detectives showed me, hoping that they'd call up some sort of response. I was smart about it then. But now . . . now what could I do? The killer was in my home!

"Think about this, Sissy. If I really wanted to put you away, do you think I'd be here talking? Do you think I'd show you how I caught you red-handed? Fuck no. I'd be at the district attorney's office, and your ass'd be in two pairs of handcuffs. Two. A pair for your wrists and a pair for your ankles. No, Sissy. I'm here for something else." Meadows put down his folder and took off his jacket. He unholstered his Glock and placed it flat on the coffee table.

"First, I should tell you that I've left an envelope in my desk that contains every detail of my discovery. Furthermore, Rosario has been transferred to Manhattan North. Captain Bartholemew agreed that he wasn't doing a good enough job with the Pink Heart murders. In fact, we concluded that he was the reason for many wasted resources of time and man-power. So Rosario is gone, and the case is in my hands. I'm supposed to assign new investigators. In plain English, I'm holding your future in my hands." Meadows laid his folder on the coffee table next to his weapon. Then he began unbuttoning his shirt.

I couldn't stop thinking about April. I couldn't help wanting to protect her. On the other hand, I had the advantage in this case . . . if I was the one to expose the killer, I was sure to be awarded with a medal, a raise and, like April suggested, a better position.

Like April suggested? Holy Moses! No wonder she wants to help me with the case. Maybe she wants to be caught. Maybe she wants me to be the one to catch her.

I had all of these assumptions, but all because of Meadows. Porky Pig just gonna march up in my apartment on a Sunday morning claimin' shit.

"Tell you what. Let's pretend that my hunch is a bunch of malarkey. I mean, I wouldn't want you to feel threatened or squeezed into a corner. I just came here to work out a . . . a business deal."

Meadows had his shirt off now and began tugging his T-shirt out of his trousers. "I could've made things difficult for you a lot sooner than this. How 'bout the stabbing victim from that domestic dispute almost two years ago? Sonoma Robbins—that name ring a bell? The woman up on Webster? Because of you freezin' up she didn't receive medical assistance in time. More important, the fucking common-law husband escaped. Your fault! Then of course there was the incident at the used car lot . . . we already discussed that. But even before you came to the 52nd, you had problems in Brooklyn. Even then, I came to the rescue. Baby, you been gettin' over like a fat rat. You're not related to no cops . . . you ain't got no clout . . ."

Meadows pulled his T-shirt off and tossed it to the side. "You definitely ain't got no money for payoffs . . . the bottom line here is that I'm your rabbi. I'm your friggin' angel of mercy. So, I was thinkin'—this bein' a dry time in my life . . . my wife has cancer . . . my kids are grown and out of the house . . . I'm a real miserable son-of-a-bitch these days. And uh . . . I kinda miss our little chemistry."

"We don't have a chemistry, you asshole. That was a one-time-only fix. And you coerced me, besides," I snapped.

"Whoa, hold on there, lady. You needed me. I helped you!"

"Well, that was then." I got up and picked up his shirt and tossed it at him.

Meadows, with his fat, flat bulldog face and extremely large body. I couldn't believe I went down on my knees for this slob with his belly like a tub. His puffy, pale arms were stained with tattoos. Not your ordinary tattoos, but detailed murals on his pink flesh. On his whole right arm was an image of the singer, Madonna; only she was crafted like a naked devil, even with the red horns, pitch forked tongue, tail, bathing in an abundance of flames. On his left arm was a tattoo of Britney Spears, also naked, except that her portrait was an innocent one; an angel with a halo and wings. It was as if this pig went to great lengths to be a billboard professing Madonna's superiority as pop-culture's sex pistol la'creme. As if this was his other function in life. His other career.

I continued, "This is now. So take your fat ass—"

Porky Pig had the Glock in his hand now. He pointed it at me with his head slanted to mean business. "Listen, you cunt. I'm calling the shots here. I wanted to make this easy for you, but I see you want problems. Okay, boom." Meadows pulled back the slide on the nine millimeter. "Here's problem number one. Assume the position."

I froze before him. My idea that this was all a dream quickly bled into reality. I couldn't wake up and make this go away.

"I said, assume the goddamned position."

I swallowed back the saliva in my mouth and knelt down between his parted legs. He already had his waistband unbuttoned and his fly unzipped. And now he pressed the nose of the Glock to my forehead. I couldn't breathe. This was it. This is how I would die.

"Let me make this simple for you, ya lil' fucker. We're gonna see each other like this once a week. You're gonna fuck me, suck me, whatever I tell ya. And you're also gonna handle a job for me here and there." He pressed harder, forcing my head back some. "It's always good to have a hit man, or a hit bitch in your case, on the job. Besides that, if I got a friend who comes to town now and then, you're gonna fuck and suck him. And I ain't gonna have no trouble outta you. Not in the least. Now. How ya like them terms?"

I was too choked up and afraid to answer. Meadows came around with his free hand and slapped my face with an open palm.

"Answer me, ya cunt! How ya like them terms?"

"O-okay. I'll do what you say. I'll do it," I said, my voice shivering.

"You betcha black ass you will. Now how 'bout a little ceremonial suck to get our new arrangement off to a bang."

THE NEXT HOUR was spent with me sucking the sergeant's dick while he used his gun to stroke my head of unmanaged hair like I was his pet. I cried as I worked my gums and tongue up and down on him. He also directed me to take his balls in my mouth, pubic hair and all.

"The next time we get it on you're gonna be some creative cunt—maybe toss my salad and suck my toes," he said. But I knew these were words to help motivate an orgasm, an orgasm that he made me swallow.

# RIVER

OUT OF CURIOSITY, I called the 52nd Precinct and asked who was in charge of the Pink Heart murders investigation. They transferred my call without notice and I got some other cop on the line. He just answered by saying, "Meadows."

"Excuse me, sir, but who's in charge of the Pink Heart murders investigation?"

"Who wants to know?"

"My name is Catrina. Catrina Brown. I'm just a local taxpayer, sir. And you never know . . . I might have some information for you."

"Is that so?" the cop said with a hearty laugh. "What sorta . . . information?"

"It's sensitive, sir. Could you tell me who's in charge?"

More laughter. Then he said, "Sissy. Sissy Dickerson's in charge. You want her phone number? Her address?"

"Is she there? Can I speak with her?"

"Do you know who this is?" said the cop, only his voice seemed to drop to a whisper. "This is Sergeant Meadows, you cunt. What're you, deranged? Now stay off my line. And I'll see you this Sunday." The line went dead.

I pulled the receiver away from my face and looked at it as if it was alive with mystery. You'll see me this Sunday?

"Crazy-ass cops," I said. And I put down the phone. Sissy Dickerson. So my fate is in her hands? A woman? I wondered just how close she was to finding me. And if I knew she was on to me, I sure had a surprise for her.

Hours later, I redialed the police station.

"Sissy Dickerson, please."

This time I wasn't transferred, but asked to hold the line. I held on for at least five minutes until the operator came back on.

"I'm sorry. Officer Dickerson is out sick today. Should I take a message?"

"No. That's fine. I'll call back."

I guess I just wanted to hear the bitch's voice. I wanted to get a feel for her. Something for me to go to sleep with . . . to dream about. I couldn't believe what was going through my mind. I'm about to kill a cop.

HIS NAME WAS Dr. Greg Pittman, a gynecologist I'd visited three or four times over the years. When I got around to it. I initially had my reservations about a male doctor touching me. But it seems like every time I turn around, men are the top of this profession or that. Dr. Pittman was reputed to be the top man in my community. The closest woman was in Manhattan, and hell if I was going all the way downtown to get my pussy checked.

It was the third visit that made me curious about Pittman, when I got to wondering if all that he was doing down there was necessary. He performed a Pap smear, with me on the table and my legs lifted apart in stirrups. He explained that he'd be "swabbing" the walls of my coochie (of course he used the word vagina) and made other small talk, it seemed, to take my mind away from his activities.

"So . . . how's the job? They treatin' you right?"

"I'm actually looking into other things. Maybe a job at the Bronx Zoo," I lied. Been there, done that.

"Hmmm . . ." he murmured and I felt the third such stroke of a Q-tip on my sugar walls.

I had been lying there with my eyes closed until I felt a subtle wind caress me. I opened my eyes to a squint and noticed that Pittman's face (his nose!) was but an inch or two away from my pussy. I said nothing. Then I heard him sniffing, and his fingers were in me, pulling my folds slightly wider apart. "This . . . this is part of the test?" I asked, not wanting to be rude.

"Well . . . it's part of the examination, dear. The

odor, if it reaches a certain intensity, is an indication of possible disease, possible infection. You never can be too sure."

I sighed, trying my best not to feel uncomfortable...

"You do seem to keep good hygiene," Pittman said. And just then one of his fingers eased into my stuff. I winced. "Everything okay?"

"Mmm-hmm," I murmured, unable to put my responses to words.

"It's important for me to . . . to search for any little sign of lesions or sores. Are you currently sexually active?"

His fingers were doubled up now, sliding in and out of me. And—shit—he expected me to answer him? I sighed; something that sounded like a hungry kitten. In and out, in and out, his fingers glided along every centimeter of my pussy. I began to writhe and wriggle and I grabbed the side of the table tight to brace myself.

"Almost done," he said.

I paid him no mind as spasms pushed through me like electric shocks. It felt good, but strange. Or is that strange, but good? Eventually I surrendered to the "examination" in its entirety.

"You like this, don't you?"

"Yes-yes-yes!" I cried out, rising and falling under his total control. His fingers on my buttons. Then, just before I climaxed, the doctor withdrew his fingers. I opened my eyes, shocked that he would stop so suddenly, wanting him to go further. Then, of course, there was that breathless, disbelieving expression on my face, with my lips parted.

"We're done here. You're in good health as far as I can see."

"Just like that?"

"Just like that. Call me for the results on the Pap smear," he said as calmly as he might say, "Pass the salt." I was delirious, but I could swear I saw Dr. Pittman pretending to pull those rubber gloves off with his teeth. A closer look and I could see him putting those fingers in his mouth like ice cream pops. I fell back against the pillow, disgusted and filled with high anxiety. I needed to get fucked. I needed the job to be completed.

I got dressed and approached the foyer that separated the doctor's examining room and reception area. There was another private office there. Dr. Pittman was now seated at a desk.

"Can I . . . can I come back later this week?"

"For what? I'm a busy man, Miss Burlington. You're scheduled for quarterly visits and you can phone in for the test results."

"I understand, but—Jesus, don't you get it? As I said this, put a grip on his shoulder.

"I need attention. I . . . I need you, Doctor Pittman. Can't you make an exception?"

"It'll cost you."

"Cost me?" I'll be damned. He's a fucking prostitute!

"That's what I said. Six hundred for a semi, a thousand for a full exam."

"Jeezus! How much for you to just look at me?" I joked, but the doctor made a face. "Okay, okay. When can I see you?" I pleaded.

"Sunday. And it'll have to be a house call. I'll see you Sunday."

Didn't that cop say that to me on the phone? I wondered if this was a good or bad omen. No matter. One thing had absolutely nothing to do with the other.

"Sunday it is."

"See you around ten-ish. And please . . . have your clothes off. I don't like to waste time with the formalities."

"I see . . . I mean, no problem," I said. And I turned away, bewildered, bewitched and between anxiety and delirium.

When I calmed down, I considered the way that Dr. Pittman handled me in his office; it was enough to make me wanna kill him. Except that he was making me feel good. Not necessarily appreciated, but, well . . . it just felt good how he used his fingers like an expert's tools. I was desperate to know how he used his other tool. That "full exam." But I was also wondering about myself. Wondering why I must be put through this. Surely I was cute enough to attract a man, a lover, without having to pay. And a thousand dollars? There was no way I could pay that kind of money. Still, I was determined to make this work. When I finished with Dr. Pittman, he'd be ready to pay me for sexual favors.

ON SATURDAY NIGHT, I turned up the volume on the stereo and danced around the apartment in nothing but panties. All I could think about was that fine Dr. Pittman. He had money and good looks, and he knew how to get me off. I honestly couldn't recall the last time I had an orgasm—one I didn't fake. But this man. Ohhhhh! He was just Mr. It.

Maybe if I could rock his world one time real good, maybe then he'll change his tune. Maybe he'll make me his woman. I could be someone to cook and clean for him, to set his clothes out the night before . . . to make him a healthy breakfast, and to be waiting for him in one of his business shirts when he returned home from a hard day's work. Of course I'd give him children; a team of boys, if he wanted. Whatever. We could even name them all after him. Greg . . . all my boys would be named Greg Pittman. They'd all grow up to be good-looking, wealthy doctors, just like their daddy.

The visions of the new Pittman family were dancing around in my mind, just as I was freestyling like some jackass trying to get attention in the middle of a nightclub. I shimmied up to a mirror, proud of my healthy breasts and my sexy leer. I pouted my lips and pretended to be looking at the new and improved River. River René Pittman. The name had more than a ring to it. It sounded like a song.

"You're gonna blow his mind, baby . . ." I blew a kiss at the mirror. "Just turn up the volume. Remember, attitude, sex appeal. Shine!"

Just as I said that I felt a presence behind me. For a split second I even saw a shadow in the mirror in front of me. I swung around. "Who's there? Who's in my house!" I crouched down and crawled toward the couch, thinking someone was behind it. Nobody. And now Brandon came running from in the kitchen. I went for my gun.

"Brandon! Good boy. You see anybody? Huh?"

With Brandon close by, I checked under the couch, in the closets, behind the curtains and in every cabinet. We looked under the kitchen sink and in the bathroom, behind the shower curtain. I even opened the front door to look down the hallway, then out of the window, up and down the fire escape. Not a soul.

"Maybe I'm seeing things, boo. Sorry, false alarm." I stroked Brandon's back. Poor thing. I must've driven him crazy, hunting around my small apartment with a loaded gun.

# APRIL

HEAVEN. THAT'S THE only word for it. I have truly been blessed to have this man in my life. He makes me feel so, so whole. Plus, I get to fill in that empty place in my heart. The one left by my late father. I just know that this is the Lord's work.

Stuart is very sexual. He likes it in many different positions and he has a number of deviant tastes. But, as the preachers all say, everyone's a sinner until they give themselves over to Christ. One day, I told myself, I'd introduce Stuart to Jesus. But not just yet. We still had so much bonding to do as lovers, and so much catching up to do as father and daughter.

"When will I get to see my daughter, April? I mean, surely you've made some kind of headway with her. It's been four months, for heaven's sake."

"Patience, Stuart, patience. I told you this is real sensitive. When I first brought it up she said no way. She was in total denial. Said she didn't even have a father."

"You didn't say that. Why didn't you tell me?"

"Because I knew that it was just a start. At least I got her talking about it. Something was better than nothing."

"I don't know if this was a good idea, April," Stuart suddenly said.

"Huh?"

"I mean . . . suppose she never wants to see me?"

"Don't be like that. It'll work out. You'll see."

"And when it does—and I know it will—what happens with us? We can't go on like this."

"Why not?"

"April, get real. If my daughter finds out I'm screwing her best friend, she'll really disown me. I'll have no hopes of uniting with my baby girl."

"You'll have me," I said, and I ran my hand over his chest. But Stuart rolled over on his side.

"That's not what I want. I want my daughter." I brushed off his comment, sure that he was speaking, not from his heart, but from a frustrated sperm donor's state of mind.

"Come on, Stuart. Lighten up. I'm sure things'll work out. Don't give up now. Not when I've come so close."

Stuart didn't respond.

"I know what can make Daddy feel better," I said. It had been at least thirty minutes since we had straight sex, but I knew how to get him excited again. I knew his body as if it were my own. I knew where to touch, where to kiss and where to nibble. We had been through this conversation once or twice before, and I was able to win his pleasure both times. Now would be no different.

I scooted down some, kissing his middle back and then his ass. I had to nudge him some so that he'd lie on his stomach, and as I predicted, he gave in. Now that he was in position, I worked my tongue over his ass cheeks, taking tiny bites to stimulate him. I was feeling stimulated just climbing over him like I was.

I divided his cheeks and finally ran my tongue along the crack of his ass until I nestled my nose where I knew he liked it. He'd taught me to bury my face where (he said) the sun don't shine. And like the A-student I was, I turned Stuart's attitude inside out. He began to moan and quiver underneath me, ordering me to freeze, to eat, to lick and to kiss at his whim. Feeling like a puppet in disguise, I followed his every instruction, and then some. When he could take no more, Stuart flipped himself over.

"Now suck it," he ordered. "Suck it, whore!"

"Yes, Daddy," I answered, knowing that the different names he liked to call me were only part of his pillow talk. Just him being kinky.

"That's right—suck it. Suck that mothafucka, you goddamn slut!"

I didn't appreciate it when Stuart used God's

name like that, but I always said a prayer immediately after the fact. I'm sure my baby would be for-
given. God forgives all. Still, I focused on satisfying
my boo. I made the noises he taught me to make,
humming like a motor so that the vibration would
make him come in my mouth. Stuart likes to come
on my face and breasts. But whenever it was left up
to me, I tried to swallow every drop. Just the thought
of having his hormones inside of my body was good
for me. It was as if I was digesting his total essence
and making him a part of me whether he accepted it
or not.

Stuart went to sleep when we were done, but
not before telling me to leave. "Take a taxi home.
I don't wanna see you for at least a week," he
said.

It made me sorta sad to be away from him for so
long, but I'd use the time to keep myself beautiful.
I could focus on next week, when I'd be twice the
fantasy. My job, as far as I was concerned, was to
keep Stuart happy.

ON THE WAY home late Saturday night, I thought
about Sissy. She seemed tense these days. The job
must've been getting to her. I was certain that
bringing her and her daddy together would impreg-
nate her with ultimate joy. It would change her life
and maybe heal a very scarred past. But then, what
about me? Both of us couldn't very well have the
same daddy. Both of us couldn't share him—not

like I was sharing him between my heart and body. My heart had a daddy. My body had a lover. And there was no way I was giving that up.

This was the Lord's will, to carry this out until whenever. So I devised a plan to keep Sissy busy thinking about a pay raise, some greater respect on her job and perhaps an award from the mayor of New York. We could accomplish all of that by digging into this Pink Heart murder investigation. Just imagine if we caught this psycho! Sissy would be Supercop and I would be the Supersleuth-slash-reporter who helped her. Wow. Maybe I'll get an award, too!

I unlocked the apartment door to find Sissy standing a few feet away from the mirror. She was in some kind of stance with her gun extended at arm's length. The gun was smoking and the mirror was broken, cracked in long, sharp splinters, with many shattered pieces on the floor underneath. She'd shot at the mirror?

"Sissy!" I shouted, with no intention to frighten her. Heck! She was frightening me! And now she shifted the gun in my direction. "Sissy, no!" I cried, afraid that a bullet would spit out at any second.

"April!" Sissy shouted, then fired shots at me. I ducked down for cover.

"Oh my God! Sissy! Why? Why are you trying to kill me? I'm sorry! Please! It's not worth it. I don't wanna die." I cried there behind the couch, afraid to move, afraid of what would happen next.

I could see the holes in the wall where Sissy had missed me. Oh God, Jesus, Lord, no! Don't let me die like this. Forgive me, Father, for I have sinned!

"Get up, bitch."

Her voice was right over me, where I had dived behind the couch. And she had that gun pointed right at my head. With my hands partially raised, I worked my way back to my feet, feeling sick and about to pee on myself.

With my lips trembling, I said, "Sissy—"

"Shut up. And I swear, if you try anything, I'll bust a cap in you so fast you'll look like a god-damned spinning top."

Tears blurred my vision some as I made sure not to execute one false move. Obviously Sissy had somehow found out about me and her father. I could also see that losing him was the least of my worries. Sissy instructed me to sit; she stood about five feet or so away with her gun at the ready.

"It was you, wasn't it? All this time. You were the killer all along . . ."

"Killer? What are you talking about?"

"Shut up. I know everything, April. You and your wigs, the trench coat—I even found this." As Sissy spoke she took another gun from the small of her back. "Where'd you get a .38 Smith and Wesson? Vicious bitch, ain't you?"

"Sissy, you are sadly mistaken," I said as I wagged my head. "I've never seen that gun before in my life."

"You're a goddamned liar, April." Sissy had both guns pointed at me now. I just knew that she was about to execute me. "I seen the pictures. There was a surveillance camera at one of the homes you went to; the photo shows you going in—trench coat and sunglasses . . ." Sissy picked up the coat and Ray-Bans and threw them in my lap. "And there's one that shows you leaving. I saw these photos with my own eyes."

"You're mistaken, Sissy. I would swear on something, but you know I don't swear."

"Oh, don't give me that born-again shit, bitch. You're a sex-starved freak, just like the rest of us. How come you been out all night? Where'd you dip to, huh? Where'd you go, Miss Abstinence? Miss 'Jesus is my Lord and Savior.' I bet you were out there suckin' somebody's dick."

"You're wrong, Sissy. You've got me all wrong! Don't say these things."

"Explain the photos. Explain the fuckin' gun, huh! How you gonna explain this?!"

Sissy squeezed off another round. It hit the couch, just by my ear. I shrieked.

"Do you know . . ." She bent closer to me; I was folded into a fetal position behind the couch. "Do you know that I had a visit from my sergeant? That he'd have your ass in cuffs behind bars if it wasn't for me?"

With my face in my hands I cried, "No, no, no . . . this can't be happening."

"You have no idea what I was put through, all because I let you move into my place." Sissy was real close now. She took my head in her hand and pressed the nose of the gun up under my chin. "I oughtta kill your black ass right here, right now. You're supposed to be my best friend!"

I couldn't say a word the way she had my face in her tight grip with that hot steel pushing up into my jaw. And I noticed we were both sweating heavily. Sobbing, and at a loss for any self-control, I managed to utter broken pleas. It felt like my last moments of life. "P-please . . . Sissy, d-don't do th-this."

Sissy pushed me, almost threw me, back against the couch and stood up again.

"Why? Give me one good reason why I shouldn't cut you down right now. Bringing a gun up in my crib? What are you gonna do? Make me another one of your victims? You killin' cops now?"

"Sissy? Is that you?" A woman's voice approached the apartment entrance. I hadn't closed the front door. "Hello?" Both Sissy and I turned our heads.

# SISSY

"EVE, YOU SCARED the shit outta me," I said as I got to my feet.

"Sorry, I— Sissy? What's the gun for? Who's home with you? I heard you arguing from all the way down the hall."

My focus was suddenly poor, with Eve's image fading in and out. I had to strain to see clearly so that she was no longer transparent.

"Sissy? You okay? Some of the neighors down the hall say they heard gunshots."

As if a powerful electrical current hit me, I jerked my head, body, then guns around to where April had been slumped over. "Oh shit! Where is she?"

"Who?"

"April, that's who. April! You come back here, dammit!" I began to rush around, jumping here and there, checking under and behind furnishings.

"Here, Eve. Take this gun. She's somewhere, and I don't want her to hurt you."

"Hurt me? Who? I—"

I pushed the .38 into Eve's palm.

"Just point and squeeze if you see her." I made an example of Eve's arms. "Point . . . and squeeze." I pressed Eve's finger harder than I expected. A shot blasted into a bookshelf.

"Oh my God!" Eve said as her body jolted.

"It's okay. It's normal to be scared the first time. But honey, there's a killer running around in my apartment. This gun will save your life."

"Killer? Why don't we just leave and call the police?"

"Eve, you're forgetting—I *am* the police. Now keep your eyes open and don't point that gun at me."

Eve shook her head and had an uncertain expression. For a few minutes, she and I crept through each room. Cabinets and closets were checked. We looked under my bed and out on the fire escape.

"Is she in there, Coco? Huh? It's okay, girl. Don't be afraid. Auntie Sissy is here to protect you. Good girl . . ."

"Shit, Sissy. Your crib must be haunted. And frankly, I'm not comfortable or safe holding any gun." Eve tossed the .38 on the couch. "And if there's a killer on the loose we should definitely be calling—"

A loud knock shook the two of us.

"Police! Open up!"

"Jesus," I grunted. Coco Puff barked from the next room.

"Thank God!" exclaimed Eve. And she didn't hesitate to go and let them in. Meanwhile, I stuffed my Glock in my waistband. Even I knew how some officers jumped to conclusions, shot first and asked questions later.

Just as Eve opened the door, I said, "Let me handle this." Then I saw Officers Arthur and Terrance Sullivan. Heckle and Jeckle.

"Dickerson? Is that you?" Both men had guns drawn.

"At almost two in the morning, it sure is. What's up?"

"What's up? Dispatch sent us. A report of shots fired came in. Possible domestic dispute."

I laughed. "Ain't that somethin'. A domestic dispute at my place." My laugh faded when I saw that Heckle and Jeckle noticed the splintered mirror. Plus, even I could smell the cordite from the spent bullets in the air.

"Oh, that," I mumbled. "Actually the shots fired were me. My gun discharged in error. I was showing my friend here how the speed loaders work, and . . . well . . . accidents happen, fellas."

"Aw, shit, Dickerson. You had us all worried," said the Sullivan with the five-o'clock shadow for a beard. He and his brother realized there was no danger and they reholstered their weapons.

The other Sullivan went to pick up my house

phone. "Gimme Dispatch please," he said after dialing a three-digit code privileged only to police officers.

"He's saving us some paperwork. You know the drill, Dickerson. Sure glad you're all right," the first twin said.

I nodded.

"Dispatch? Yeah, Terrance Sullivan . . . Sandra? Hey, wassup? That call for shots fired, is there a trace on the caller? No? Okay . . . mark it as a false alarm, would ya? And if you hear that voice again, tell the caller to cut it out 'fore we take 'em downtown and throw away the key."

"Hey, Terry, pass me that."

"Sandra? Hold on. Arthur wants to holler at cha." One brother passed the receiver to the other.

"Sandy? Yeah, Arty. I was wonderin' if we could do breakfast . . ."

While Terry, Arty and Sandy made their respective remarks, I gave Eve a reassuring eye. But she was spellbound by all of this. How informal things were in light of all that just transpired. She was probably thinking, Gunshots. A killer on the loose. Breakfast with Sandy? Wow, I must be dreaming.

"Hey, Dickerson, you'd better clean up that broken mirror before somebody cuts themselves."

"Will do, Terry."

"And good morning to you, ma'am," said Arty, tipping his hat at Eve. Then they left.

"I don't know what the hell is going on around here, Sissy, but—"

"Help me with this mirror. You heard the man. Somebody might get cut."

Eve made an exasperated sound with her lips. A sound a horse might make.

"What brings you by my place anyway, Eve? Isn't Saturday night busy at the Lucky Love?"

"There's a promoter renting the club tonight. They got some kind of exotic female dance review goin' on, and I told my boss before I wasn't workin' them nights."

"You don't like coochie all of a sudden?"

"Very funny, Sissy. It's just that the dancers get the men all hot and excited. And when the show's over, most of 'em come and try to hit on the bar-tender, 'cause I'm, like, the only female who still got somethin' left for their imaginations."

"Hmmm. That is funny. A club full of horny men. All with miserable home lives . . . wives are probably home alone singin' the blues."

"I'm sure," said Eve.

"So you came to see me? Here? You know I got a housemate. We can't do nothin' here."

Eve looked around, then said doubtfully, "I guess."

"She's just out, Eve. Some women do fuck men, ya know?"

"Sometimes I think you're just playin' me, Sissy,

keepin' me away from your place so your options will be open for other lovers."

"Stop it, Eve. First of all, you and I have no formal strings attached. We're only fucking. We ain't married, babe."

Eve stopped sweeping pieces of mirror into the dustpan I held.

"I'm sorry, Eve. I didn't mean it that way. You know I have strong feelings for you. If I didn't, believe me, we wouldn't be bumpin' bushes, and I certainly wouldn't have my tongue all in your stuff."

"Damn, Sissy. You put things so bluntly. I hate loving you sometimes."

"And you're gonna hate this, too. You gotta go. I have a bone to pick with April, my housemate. Some shit we gotta discuss."

"Mmm-hmm . . ."

"I might even be kicking her out of here."

"Huh?" Eve swung back around, to face me again. "Are you serious?" she asked hopefully.

"Serious as two fat ladies sharing the same life preserver."

Eve jumped on me, hugging me like we hadn't seen each other in years.

"What's the big deal?"

"Sissy, I need you. That's the big deal. You're like my big sister. But you're also my lover. I hate being away from you. I hate it." Eve's face was nestled in the crook of my neck and there was the delicate heat, her exhales warming my skin.

"Okay, babe. Seriously. Get yourself together. You gotta go."

"Can I see you tomorrow night?" she asked.

I nodded.

I FINALLY GOT to sleep at three o'clock. But instead of a peaceful rest, I found myself struggling with all of the many images, the evening's events repeating themselves like a group of half-hour television sitcoms playing all at once. Sergeant Meadows starred in one, along with his costars Madonna and Britney Spears. There was a fierce battle going on, with Madonna singing *Like a Virgin* while trying to slug it out with Britney, who was singing "*Oops! . . . I Did It Again*" as she ducked and returned punches herself. The winner of the battle, according to the menagerie in my head, would get a first opportunity to stick Meadows with a newly sharpened pitchfork. Then, of course, Madonna and Britney would take another shot at that deep tongue kiss they once staged for television. This time, it would be for real.

Another sitcom starred Maritza and me, where we teamed up to avenge all the battered housewives of the Bronx. Lots of them. The two of us were on a hill in all of our police regalia, holding military assault weapons while a sea of angry men charged toward us. Like two female Rambos, Martiza and I shot them down. When it was over, their blood made a murky red sea that I eventually drowned in.

The last sitcom starred April, the Pink Heart Murderess. I was chasing her up and down the streets of the Bronx. Both of us were naked; she with her .38, me with my Glock 9. We went on like this tirelessly until the sidewalks were crowded with an audience of male spectators. It wasn't long before I realized that these were the men April had killed, all standing along our path like some kind of zombies with missing limbs, penises, ears and noses. I noticed that one guy had no eyelids, with blood-soaked cheeks. Another had his eyeballs extracted—severed optic nerves hung down onto his cheeks. Of course, there were the gunshot victims, too. All told, it was a gross scene; a nightmare really. But it raced past me in a blur as I continued to chase April. Just as I was about catch her, I heard a noise.

# RIVER

I DREAMED OF Dr. Greg Pittman. God! It was like we already did it. Like we already fucked. All I could think about were his familiar hands caressing my curves, his body on top of mine and him plugging his dick into my hungry holes. I figured Doc to have a big dick too, because he was so tall. Tall and handsome, with his own practice. What more could I need in life?

All morning Brandon nagged me, following me around my place, probably thinking I'd let him lick me. I told him no, that I was saving myself for the good doctor. And it had been that way for days now. I wanted to be sure I gave him something unsatisfied and hungry. There were nights and days I've wanted to touch myself, but I held back. It was as simple as mind over matter. I kept envisioning the big picture

Me, Mrs. Greg Pittman. From now on it was

gonna be gynecology seminars, medical conven-
tions and beating off the sluts who would come
around for attention from my man. Oh, hell no.
That part of the game was gonna come to an end
before it ever started. I'd put my life on it.

For the doctor, I made myself look real appeal-
ing in a nice silk teddy. I pulled my hair back into
a bouncing ponytail and I went with no makeup.
Some of my past lovers have claimed how I was
lucky to need no makeup . . . that I woke up beautiful. I hoped Doc would feel the same.

The knock at the door made me jump. I was so
full of anticipation, I could've exploded.

"Come on, Brandon. No time to get jealous
now. Take your golden ass in the room. Come on!"
There was no way a dog was gonna mess up my
long-awaited fuck. I locked the door, not expecting
to see Brandon for at least two hours. Maybe
longer. Then I skipped to the front door. I didn't
even bother to look through the peephole. I just
snatched the door open and put on my most radiant
smile.

"I see you've been waiting for me!"

"You're not—" the doctor.

A portly, bearded white man I'd never seen before stepped over the threshhold, shut the door behind him and swung around to smack me square
across the face with his meaty palm. "Now let's get
this party started," he said as I fell back to the floor.

"We can get this over with right quick if you just keep your mouth shut and do what the fuck I say"

He reached down and grabbed under my arms and dragged me toward the couch. "I would tape your goddamned mouth shut, but I wanna hear you cry and moan when I fuck you in your ass." He began to undo his belt as he said this. I was petrified. This stranger who had pushed his way into my apartment was about to rape me!!?? At first I was afraid. Shocked at how he manhandled and assaulted me. But somewhere in my adrenaline rush I become excited by the fear. The smack was nothing. That shit just made my heart jump around. But fuck! I was flabbergasted by the idea that this stranger was literally asking to be my next victim. This was the type of mothafucka I loved to fuck and then kill.

I thought about my guns. I knew that my .38 was in the bedroom, out of reach. But the loaded Magnum? Now that baby was stuffed between the cushions of my couch for just this sort of occasion.

"Might as well assume the position. Let me see that nice round ass of yours . . ."

I had to think fast. First of all, this man was fucking up my appointment with the doctor. And, second, there was absolutely no way this guy was stickin' anything in my ass. He got me mixed up with the next bitch.

"Listen, mister . . . No sense in forcin' things.

Why don't you lemme get you nice and hard before you put it in. I mean, I've never been raped before . . . but wouldn't you like me to be nice n' wet before you . . . you know."

"Oh. Good thinkin'. I guess I'd still have my rape fantasy, wouldn't I?"

"Of course, mister. I won't let you down. Now why don't you let me get my hands on that thing and get it ready?"

"Now you're talkin'," he said, now with his pants at his ankles. "I thought that was pretty cute of you to call my office the other day, actin' like you're a taxpayer with info about the killer."

I pretended to understand the man as I took his limp penis in my hand and massaged his hairy balls. Info about the killer? What the fuck was he talkin' about?

"And what'd you say your name was? A Ms. Brown? Catrina was it? So that's your new name? 'Cause I like the idea. This way it keeps our relationship on the top-secret level. Now how 'bout suckin' me, Miss Catrina Brown."

"Okay. But I can start from the back? Can you kneel on the couch for me and let me work my tongue around? I'll make sure I eat every inch of you," I offered with determination in my eyes and tone of voice.

"Wow, Dickerson—I mean, Catrina. You are a superfreak, for real!" As he said this he got on all fours, facing away from me, with his naked, hairy ass inches from my face.

"Okay, woman . . . get to eatin' "

It took me less than three seconds to feel around under the cushions for my .357, and less than one to shove the barrel of the gun straight up this stranger's ass. Blood splashed me. And the heavy man roared in agony upon penetration of the Magnum. But it was just the beginning of what I had in store for him.

"Yeah. I'm a freak. But I'm a living freak"—I squeezed off two gunshots up into his asshole; his entire body proved to be an effective silencer— "And you're a dead one." I finished saying as I watched the man's convulsions, followed by some violent shaking and eventual lifelessness.

I dragged and rolled my latest victim from the living room into the room where Brandon was. So I hurried to tidy things up, flipping the cushions on the couch to hide the bloodstains. Then I jumped into the shower to get all fresh and clean again. I couldn't help thinking how this fool came to me. As though he had a death wish. And while my thoughts raced, I knew that the good doctor would be arriving at any minute.

The phone rang.

"Hello?"

"Sissy? It's Eve."

I said, "Sorry, wrong number." And I hung up.

The phone rang again. Nuisance bitch. I picked up the receiver, set it back down without answering. Then I took the receiver back off the hook and set it on the table. I didn't have time to play telephone operator. You got the wrong number, bitch. Get a phone book.

I only hoped that Dr. Pittman wouldn't try to call me to, maybe, cancel the date. Finally, there was the knock at the door, one which I'd been patiently waiting for. There was a slight perspiration under my arms and I felt slippery between my legs.

"Hold on! Be right there!" I shouted melodically and grabbed up the closet piece of assistance: a kitchen towel. I dabbed underneath my arms and between my legs. I sprayed myself with Orange Blossom Mist. I also sprayed some in the air around the apartment to help hide the fact that there was a dead body in the next room. Once I reached the door, this time, I made sure to use the peephole before opening the door. Thank God it was him, because the next person who tried to interfere with my morning was gonna get a bullet between the eyes, never mind getting it up the ass.

"Doc!" I welcomed him with my best electric greeting.

"River. Good to see you," he said, and he allowed my hug.

I kissed his cheek and stepped aside for him to pass me. Mmm-mmmmmm, I'm gonna tear that ass up, I told myself. Then I triple-locked the front door. "A drink, Doc? Something to unwind to?"

He unzipped his leather jacket and I hurried to take it. From this moment on, it would be house-wife skills all the way.

"Actually, to be perfectly honest with you, this is a house call for me, darling. I have a busy sched-ule today, as you might imagine. So, if you don't mind . . ." Dr. Pittman gave me the eyes. Let's get down to it, River.

Wow. He was so certain, so confident about his objectives. "Well . . . you're the doctor," I said ner-vously. "So, where do we begin?"

"It looks like you've already gotten yourself prepared."

"I guess. Can you blame a girl for knowing what she wants?" I shrugged and showed a childish guilt on my face. It was an expression that usually sold other men, so I figured Doc would be no different.

But he didn't seem affected.

He just said, "Right." And then added, "Shall we get the business out of the way first?"

Oh shit. I didn't expect to be put on the spot like this. I figured I'd put it on him so good that maybe he'd wanna pay me . . . that he'd overlook the money end of this little get-together. "You're real serious about this money thing, aren't you? I mean, can't we deal with the business later? It makes things so cut and dried. Takes the passion out of the occasion, don't you think?"

Dr. Pittman crossed his arms and rolled his eyes. "Miss Burlington? Are you wasting my time? I have a busy day ahead, didn't I say that? Women are standing by their doors at this very moment, cash in hand. What makes you so different?"

Already, my fantasy was falling apart; melting right before my very eyes. This was so unexpected, and not at all what I imagined. I felt like crying.

"Oh . . . now with the pout and the tears. Listen . . ." Pittman reached for his jacket. "I'm not the doctor you need. Dr. Wise is a psychologist. Dr. Simmons is a therapist. They have office hours like I do." His jacket was on now. I could already feel him leaving the apartment before the act. "Why don't you call them and handle your emotional problems? I'm not the one."

My tears were steady now. "All right! You want money?" I marched over to my cookie can on the kitchen counter. I snatched it up and reapproached him. "Here! Take it, you bastard!"

"What's this?"

"It's all the money I have, that's what it is."

He opened the can to find bunches of dollar bills that I had accumulated as a result of dancing topless at the Five and Dime, a club over in the South Bronx.

"This, you call money? This can't be more than three, four hundred tops. You agreed to a thousand."

"Please, Doc. Please! I beg you. Take my savings. I'll pay you the rest. I swear to God, I will.

Just please . . . don't leave. Don't leave me this way . . ." Before I knew it, I was down on my knees, my hands brushing up and down the sides of his thighs. I was that desperate. More so than I could control.

"Let me show you, Greg. Let me show you I'm the only one you need . . . let me prove to you that I can fulfill your fantasies . . . your dreams . . ." I had gotten so far as to unfasten his pants before he pushed me away.

"God, please don't leave me like this. I need you. And I know you'll need me. I'll do whatever you ask. I'll be your slave. Just say it . . ." I could hear myself spinning out of control, with my tears soaking into the silk of my lingerie.

Dr. Pittman crouched down near me. He lifted my face from the floor where I had been slumped over like a baby. "Keep your money and get some help, River. 'Cause you are one—sick—woman." He stood back up and turned toward the door. "How do I get this thing unlocked?" he asked while he played with the different locks.

As he tried to make sense of my maze, there was enough time for me to get to the couch. I wasn't playing anymore. I was determined to have my cake and eat it, too.

"You don't get it unlocked, Doc. Not till we're done here."

"Shit! What're you—put that down before I call the police," he said with his hands on his hips.

"Oh really? Now, ahh . . ." I reached for the phone and jerked the cord out of the wall jack.

"How do you intend to do that? Are you gonna send a message in a bottle? Or ahh . . . how about a homing pigeon? Or, ahh . . . I know. You can make a fire and send smoke signals. Yeah! That's it, Doc. A fire!"

"You have now, one hundred percent, flipped your lid, woman. Now please, do not point that gun at me!"

"Point it? Shit, Doc. I think I might use it!" I shot a round in Pittman's direction, but deliberately missed, purposely hitting a painting hanging by the front door. The sound of the Magnum was defeating.

"Oh my God! You're fuckin' crazy!"

"You ain't seen crazy, Doc," I said, as I backed away into the kitchen. I still had the gun pointed at him, and we were close enough for me to keep him as a target and turn on the gas stove at the same time.

"What are you doing?! You're gonna kill us."

"Not exactly, Doc. See, the way I figure it, if you hurry and get your clothes off . . . and if you come and fuck me . . . if you let me bear your child, there should be just enough time for us to leave here alive. Otherwise, I don't wanna live."

"Oh Jesus!" he hollered with pie-wide eyes.

"No, no. Jesus ain't got shit to do with this, boo. It's just me and you . . . or would it be proper

English to say you and I? Well . . . anyway . . . the gas should already be oozing into the air so we don't have long. What's it gonna be?"

"Okay, Goddamnit! You want it that bad, I'll give it to you. You're a goddamned freak of nature!" He growled like an animal.

"Oh, but, Greg. You shouldn't talk that way about the mother of your son! Your future wife. Now . . . hurry with the pants . . . lemme have that monster of yours!"

He moved ever faster, and was now standing in boxers. Red boxers with little yellow hearts printed all over. I was reminded of the sunflowers on Jethro's shorts. Doc kept looking at the stove.

"Can a girl get a bare-chested man? How 'bout it?"

I was seated on the couch—a couch that would eventually reek of the new blood and semen. Less semen, if I could keep it all inside of me. Doc hustled out of his shirt and was eventually standing in shorts and socks.

"Good. Good. Now, come to Momma. Come put that monster in Momma's mouth. Momma knows how to make him stand up." I could smell the gas getting thicker in the kitchen, easing into the living area.

"Better hurry," I said, holding the Magnum in my lap and waiting to receive Greg Jr.

"Mmmm . . ." As best I could, I said, "I like . . . I like . . ." And I continued to moan, causing a vibration with him inside of my mouth. "What's wrong baby? Greg Junior won't stand up?"

"Jesus! Can we just—Aaargh!" Doc let out an aggravated yell.

"I know what you like. Let River take care of these two . . ." I slurped at Jason's balls, he eventually grew hard. "Abracadabra! Now, I'll just get on the couch . . . go ahead and give it to me, Daddy. Make me your wife . . . uuuh!"

I felt him, finally. He grabbed my love handles and pounded me from behind as I looked over my shoulder at him. Our bodies slapped skins until he continuously filled me and hurt me at the same time. The friction was rough and it grew rougher. I felt the gun slip out of my hand as I cried Greg's name deliriously.

"Yes! Greg, Yes! Spank me, Greg. Take me! I know you'll learn to love me . . . I'll make you love me . . . Take it . . . YES! YES!!" I was being pounded hard, then soft, then not at all. I swear I came three times already. And now I was exhausted on the couch; I wasn't sure if he came inside of me.

"Dumb bitch."

I turned my head up to see Greg with the Magnum pointed at me.

"I should shoot you where you lay!" Then he opened the chamber, allowed the bullets to fall on the floor and dropped the gun. He pulled his pants on, ignored his shirt and grabbed his jacket before rushing to the door.

"Oh no you don't," I yelled, diving for the gun and scrambling for bullets to load. One was all I needed. I aimed. I fired. I saw a flash and then an even greater light, bright like the sun. I felt extreme heat all over my face and body. I was on fire, but somehow there was nothing I could do about it. The last thing I saw was an outline of Greg, as though he had stepped into the sun.

# APRIL

"ALL RISE! THE honorable Judge Florence Williams Baker presiding."

"Please be seated," the judge announced. "In the matter of the United States of America versus Sissy Dickerson, we will now hear the closing arguments starting with you, Mr. Moynihan. And please, sir, let's not replay this entire trial from start to finish. I'm certain that the jury has a clear understanding of all the elaborate details presented during the past two months. So if you would, please make your points and let's wrap this up. That goes for you too, Mr. Quinn. I'm sure I speak for our jurors when I say that this has been a long, grueling trial . . . one that we'd like to put behind us. And of course the ladies and gentlemen of the jury would like to return home to their families." Judge Baker nodded toward the jury, evoking a few smiles and overall relief.

I leaned over to whisper in my attorney's ear. Mr. Quinn sure was a nice man; too nice, I thought, to be so deliberate and aggressive during my trial.

"How does he get to go first?" I asked.

"We decided on it in the judge's chambers," Mr. Quinn said.

"You mean, you all actually get to sit in with her? Is the stenographer there, too?"

"Most times, no. But trust me, Ms. Dickerson, I was looking out for your best interests."

"Okay. But I wish you all would stop calling me Sissy Dickerson. My name is April. April Davis. How many times must I tell you?"

"Of course. I'm sorry, ma'am. You just relax and let the professionals handle things. Trust me— you're in very good hands, ahh . . . Miss Davis."

I smiled and said, "Thank you." It was good to know at least somebody got it right.

"LADIES AND GENTLEMEN of the jury, as Judge Williams said, this has indeed been a lengthy trial. And I thought I'd speak on behalf of the government and the people of the United States when I offer you the most sincere thanks for your time and attention. Most important, thank you for taking time out from your busy lives and your families, to join us in making a decision about this particularly bloody, horror-filled case. That being said, I want to remind you that this is a capital murder case. I want to remind you that we're not here only to determine the future of Miss Sissy Dickerson, but we're also here to achieve closure for thirty-two families. That's two and three times as many sons and daughters . . . and perhaps many more friends and extended family members than any of us can claim.

"Yes, we're here to resolve a matter that those hundreds of people have had to live with for the past two or three years. And inevitably, we are all here to fulfill the purpose set forth by the laws of our land. And this may even supercede those laws when you consider one of our oldest laws: the Fifth Commandment proclaims, 'Thou shalt not kill.' And it is here today that we must affirm that age-old mandate thirty-two times over . . .

"Let's not lose perspective. This woman, the defendant, Sissy Dickerson, is, dare I say, the most lethal weapon of this century. She is a one-woman army. Oh, don't let the image fool ya. I'm right here with you every day, looking over at this table, at this fairly attractive woman who was part of our police force, who set out to protect and serve the good people of New York. But after so much testimony . . . after we've heard about the deathbed confession . . . after we've reviewed the psychiatric evaluations and listed to some of the country's foremost professionals of varying mental disorders . . . we now know unequivocally, that this woman is far from compassionate, far from the picture that's been painted of a person with a personality disorder.

The woman who you see before you is nothing but chaos on two feet! She's an intelligent, well-spoken, calculating killing machine! She's not just a cop-killer, for God's sakes! She's a people-killer!

"She is not only calculating, but she premeditates before she kills. Who among us can ever forget the testimony of Miss Bonnie Witherspoon? Who was forced at gunpoint to watch this woman . . . this . . . thing terrorize Mr. Jethro Benjamin and Mr. Freddie Cox, who later killed himself as a result of Miss Dickerson's threats on his life. Who among us can forget how the defendant earned access to these victims under the disguise of police officer, only to return later to sever their limbs, as in the case of Mr. Victor Hightower on Pelham Parkway, or as with George Webb, who was found with his head decapitated having been hacked to death with an axe.

"Calculated, ladies and gentlemen. A ruthless, heartless devil on two feet. That's who really sits before us this day to be judged by you fine, tax-paying citizens.

"And is there anyone who can forget the testimony of Mr. Stuart Dickerson? This man, who the defense has so melodramatically painted as a sex fiend—an incestuous father—a child abuser—has gone out of his way to come before you to face certain false claims and lies. He came here as a tax-paying citizen, like you and me, who just wants the best for his daughter. But on the other hand, he has made the ultimate sacrifice that a father can make. He has told the world that his daughter, Sissy Dickerson, is a pathological liar, that she is a remarkable practitioner of deceit and that she ultimately must be removed from society in order for others to be safe. In most cases, it's the parent who will go to any extent to lie on behalf of a child. But Mr. Dickerson's testimony is evidence that he cares about people . . . about their safety. He too wants the killings to stop.

"Ladies and gentlemen. Sissy Dickerson has fed men to the lions at the Bronx Zoo. She has bitten the penises off of a number of her victims. She's bludgeoned her victims with heavy objects, with machetes and meat cleavers. She's used electric saws and—need I go on? Sissy Dickerson, in a nutshell, is a cannibalistic menace to society. And I believe the people have shown you, the jury, beyond a reasonable doubt that Sissy Dickerson knew exactly what she was doing, when and how and why. She should not only be removed from society, but also from the world as we know it. Sissy Dickerson, ladies and gents, is the devil in disguise."

"Are you quite through, Mr. Moynihan?"

"Indeed, Your Honor. Thank you."

"Then I believe we should have a half hour recess to clear our minds and we shall return to hear the closing statements of the defense." Judge Williams slammed her hammer.

"All rise!"

We did as the court clerk asked, and the judge left the bench and courtroom as if wearing roller skates.

"What happens now?" I asked my lawyer, knowing that there were three uniformed goons behind me, about to escort me somewhere.

"The plan hasn't changed, dear. You're doing an excellent job with the innocent expression. I think the jury is buying it. An actress couldn't have done it any better."

"But I'm not acting, Mr. Quinn. I *am* innocent!" I exclaimed.

"Okay, okay. Please keep your voice down. Don't forget what we talked about. Courtroom ethics."

"But the jury will believe us, won't they? I mean, I've always trusted in the justice system and the Lord."

"Well, you keep it up. Keep the faith, Miss . . . Davis. We're gonna win this, you hear me?"

"And then I can go home? I can return to my friend Sissy? And her dog, Coco Puff? And I can go back to my freelance writing?"

"Yes, of course. Of course you can. Eventually everything will be normal again."

"You wouldn't lie to me, would you? I mean, you know what they say about lawyers, don't you?"

"Don't believe anything others say."

"Do you believe in Jesus, Mr. Quinn? Do you believe He will make things right again?"

"Of course. Now go with the gentlemen here

and do some of that meditating you told me about." They were already tugging at my arms.

"Prayer, sir. I don't meditate, I pray."

"Right, right. I'll see you in thirty minutes."

"Thank you. God bless," I said.

The guards escorted me out of the courtroom, through a side door and into a holding cell. I had handcuffs and shackles on the whole time. I was also wearing a pink dress that Mr. Quinn gave me. It was a bit old-fashioned and it smelled like it had been hanging in some kind of storage somewhere. But I agreed to wear it on account of Mr. Quinn explaining how the color pink on a woman was supposed to curry favor from the eight women on the jury. He also said he hoped at least two men on the jury were attracted to me, that it would make his job a whole lot easier.

"Here's somethin' for you to read," barked the court officer as he tossed a *New York Post* through the bars of the holding cell. I heard his belly laugh as he walked away.

JUDGMENT DAY NEARS FOR

PINK HEART MURDERESS

Sissy Dickerson faces certain death

after a two-month trial.

*By Wallace Reed.*

BRONX, NY, July 28 (AP)—There is so much mystery surrounding the woman being tried for the series of killings known as The Pink Heart murders that there is even uncertainty over whether her name is really Sissy Dickerson.

"That was the name she used to join the police academy. Then, of course, there is her father by the same last name," said Captain Bartholemew, the commander and chief at the 52nd Precinct where Ms. Dickerson worked for more than two years.

So far, investigators have come up with one alias, April Davis. It is said that it is April Davis who has been on trial for most of these past two months and not Sissy Dickerson, since the renowned psychotherapist, Janice Mifflin, Ph.D, who was brought to the stand testified that Ms. Dickerson had the severe condition known as multiple personality disorder, or MPD.

"Individuals with MPD experience themselves as more of an 'us' than 'I'. They possess separate identities, each with a unique sense of self, and sometimes including differences in age, gender and race," said Mifflin, who in addition to being the one of the nation's foremost experts on neuroscientific research, is also a dean at Connecticut's Barraca University and Seabrook Institute where she continues her research on brain study and the human mind.

"These alter-personalities (as opposed to alter-egos) often have different ways of speaking, acting and relating to the world. One alter-personality may be right handed, while another is left handed. One may require reading glasses, while another has no problem with fine print."

If what Mifflin says applies to Sissy Dickerson,

defendant in one of the biggest serial killing sprees since David "Son of Sam" Berkowitz, then clearly, it is a mystery who this woman really is. It is also a mystery how many more aliases or victims there are as a result of this woman's actions.

The national spotlight is now focused on the outcome of this trial, with law enforcement experts amazed at how this woman almost got away with murder thirty-two times. "If not for her setting off that gas explosion, we might still be stumped and frustrated to this day," added Captain Bartholemew.

No one knows for sure how many cases exist that mirror Ms. Dickerson's; however, it is a general opinion that Bronx residents are sleeping a lot easier these days with her behind bars.

The U.S. Attorney in this case, Bobby Moynihan, contends that Sissy Dickerson knows exactly what she's doing, and what she's done.

"She is the master of disguise, using wigs and sunglasses to hide her true identity over the years." Moynihan is puzzled as to why and how Dickerson came to dispense with such violence and horrors.

Dr. Mifflin says, "One of the most extreme consequences of severe childhood abuse is MPD, the essential feature of which is severe discontinuities in the unification or integration of consciousness, identity and memory."

If child abuse was in fact an element of Ms. Dickerson's past, then that would call into question the motives of her father, Stuart Dickerson, who appeared on the stand weeks ago and who ultimately damaged his daughter's defense, so say legal experts. In any event, closing arguments are scheduled for today, where proceedings are likely to recall images and testimonies of one of the most vicious, most violent murder sprees in this country's history.

AS LONG AS I've been a freelance writer, with my work published in a number of national newspapers and magazines, I've never before seen so much misinformation. How could they call Sissy a murderer? I mean, if there's anyone who knows who she is it should be me, her best friend . . . her housemate. The stuff this staff writer put in the *Post* was so wrong and couldn't have been further from the truth. Sissy is a good person. She's law-abiding. And for goodness sakes, she's a police officer. Like, protect and serve. Hello?!

For two months we had been on trial, where they were trying to pin a bunch of murders on me and Sissy, and still I had yet to see some hard evidence. They said that Sissy and I were the same person and that we switched roles now and then. Something called MPD, like the writer put in the newspaper. But my lawyer had to keep me from laughing in this otherwise serious proceeding. I'm supposed to sit there in the courtroom while these folks lie on me? I could only pray that God would make things right, and that justice was, as they say, blind considering how I'm a black woman and all.

It's a good thing they allowed Sissy and me to share the same cell back at Riker's Island. This way we get to discuss our own opinions on the trial. The only thing is, I know she's mad about me and her father. She hasn't said anything yet, but I can feel her anger. Call it a woman's intuition. One day soon, I'd have to come clean about the whole relationship between Stuart and me. I don't know what got into me—the devil, surely—to go and think I could take her father from her. To think I could keep it all a secret. Again, I'd have to leave it to God.

# SISSY

**WHEN I HEARD** the court officers laughing, I had to ask what the joke was.

"Here's your newspaper back. I honestly don't see what's so funny. Aren't we supposed to be on the same side? Enforcing law and order and whatnot?"

One of the officers, the short balding one with the bushy eyebrows and the tub of a belly, said, "Are you serious?" as he accepted the newspaper through the bars. "Did you even read this?" He poked at the article about "JUDGMENT DAY."

"I did. But I could've gotten that kind of bullshit out of the *National Enquirer*. I mean, do you boys honestly believe that crap? Me? More than two personalities? I can hardly deal with my own problems, yet they say I live dual lives."

"To be frank witcha, it's not really my call, sweetheart. But you can't help but to wonder, ya know?

Like . . . who are you now? Who were you ten minutes ago?"

"You're lookin' at me, ain't you? Do I look crazy? I'm the most solid person at the 52nd."

"Were . . . you were the most solid person. You're the most solid person behind bars, now."

"Yeah. Until the decision comes in. I gotta trust the law. I mean, I spent years enforcing it. Now it's time for me to cash in."

"Oh, yer gonna cash in, all right."

"What's that supposed to mean? Can you believe this guy, April? Just straight disrespectful. And to think I wanted to—"

"Hey fellas! She's doin' it again!"

"Come on back over here, Patrick, before you start talkin' to yourself, too," another officer called out.

"Listen, babe. I gotta get back to the desk. But ahh . . . you two sit tight. You'll be heading back into the courtroom any time now."

"Yeah. Thanks a lot," I said. And the three jerks went on laughing about my fate.

"The eyes of the blind shall see out of their gloom and darkness," said April.

"April, I told you I'm not interested in being cooped up with you if you're gonna keep on with your Bible talk. You're driving me crazy."

"Sorry."

"No, I'm sorry. You should've never been caught

up in all of this. If I hadn't brought you in as a housemate, you wouldn't be here right now."

"Yeah, but I'm glad I'm here, Sissy. At least you have a true-blue friend to share this challenge with."

"True blue," I said with a raised eyebrow. "You're not serious, are you?"

"I knew you'd wanna talk about that, Sissy."

"I bet you did."

April scooted over on the bench so that she was within arm's reach. Close enough for me to reach out and smack the shit out of her for betraying me.

"Could you at least listen to me? Hear me out before you start judging?"

I folded my arms and looked away. Why do those guards keep staring over here?

"Sissy, I'm sorry. From deep down . . . from the bottom of my heart. I was wrong. You have every right to be angry with me. It's just . . . well, I never had a father. And then, well . . . when I met him, I just got greedy. I just wanted him all to myself. I wanted to know what it was like to have a daddy. I wanted to feel loved and protected and taught. I wanted to feel secure like all the other girls with daddies. Even if it was for a short time, even if you found out, I felt it would be worth it. It was my once-in-a-lifetime opportunity. And just how many of us get to realize our hopes and dreams? All my life I dreamed of Daddy. I wondered what he looked like . . . what his voice sounded like . . . what it would be like to be touched by him."

"And he sure did touch you, didn't he? Don't think I can't read between the lines, April. Don't think I don't know what went on between you two. All your tears and crying can't undo what you did. You took my father right from under my nose, then you fucked him, and all the while you're lookin' me in the face every day like everything is all peaches and cream."

"Oh Sissy—" April wailed with her face cupped in her hands. "I'm so sooorry. I was so wrong. I did the worst thing to betray you."

Now I was crying. Shit.

"It was the only way I could hold on to him. He was about to . . . he was gonna try and meet you. He—"

"Damn, April. Couldn't you just go for it after we met? Not that you'd be any more of a saint than you already are. But at least you wouldn't have violated our relationship. I mean, how many of us can claim true friends? After we cut off this one and let go of that one, what else is left? It's like, you invent all of this time, all of these emotions and convictions—oh, you're the best friend a girl could have! And for what? What's it all worth if you can't be faithful? If you can't maintain allegiance?"

April looked up at me with tearstained cheeks. "Could you ever forgive me, Sissy? I mean, who are we if we can't forgive each other for mistakes? I was wrong. I know this. I don't know what got into me. I mean, I know who . . . but I . . . I must've . . . I wasn't myself. I was possessed by the little girl in me. The little girl who missed Daddy."

"And who were you possessed by to make you go and fuck him? Huh, April?"

"I was weak, Sissy. I had no discipline. I was lonely. I—"

"He was so handsome up on the stand. Was that how he looked when you met him?"

"Oh Sissy . . . you had to be there. He was dashing and cavalier and gentlemanly. He was the man of my dreams."

"Yeah, and he'll be something else too, once I win this trial. Did you hear the stuff he said up there on the stand? Lying bastard!"

April said nothing. I looked her in the eyes, wondering if there was anything left to us. Wondering if we had a connection.

"I need to speak with my client," a voice said from some distance away. I looked over to see our lawyer, Mr. Quinn, signing a book and being admitted through a metal detector.

"Ms. Davis?"

"Wrong again, Mr. Quinn. I'm Ms. Dickerson. She's Miss Davis," I told him.

"Yes, yes, of course," the attorney said, shaking his head as if to free himself of cobwebs. "Actually it's good that I can talk to you. I need to ask you a very, very personal question, Sissy. And I need you to be one hundred percent truthful with me."

"Now what kind of cop would I be if I went around tellin' lies?"

For a time, Mr. Quinn was silent. Then he said, "Sissy, why did your father leave home?"

"Mr. Quinn, that was more than twenty years ago."

"I know, I know. But think, Sissy. And please, please be honest. This means everything to our case."

I looked Mr. Quinn in the eyes, then I looked down to the floor. I was at a loss for words. Of course I knew, but why did we have to talk about it? What did it have to do with this trial?

"Miss Dickerson?" He came as close to the cell bars as he could. Then he said, "He abused you, didn't he? Your father sexually abused you, your mother found out and ordered him to leave, isn't that the case?"

"No."

"She threatened to go to the police, to lock him up—"

"No. You're wrong."

"And even the men in the neighborhood . . . they threatened to beat him up, didn't they?"

"No! No! Nooo!"

"Miss Dickerson, you may not have seen your father in two decades, but he wants you to fry so his sex crimes don't surface, right?" Quinn growled.

I felt myself sink to the cold cell floor. "No, Daddy, please . . . I'll do what you ask. Just please don't hurt me again. Don't beat me. I'll be a good girl . . . no, I won't tell Mommy . . . no, I won't tell the teachers. I love you, Daddy. I'll always love you. Forever."

I heard Mr. Quinn say, "My God." Then he left me and said, "Guards, please be kind to her. I beg of you. The woman is very sick. Very, very sick."

"ALL RISE! THE honorable Judge Florence Williams Baker presiding."

"Be seated. Can we have the jury back, please?"

The court clerk opened a side door for the jurors to return to their seats.

"We're about ready to hear your closing arguments, counselor."

"Thank you, Your Honor," Mr. Quinn began. "And thank you, fine citizens, for your patience over these past two months. It has indeed been a long, grueling trial. No need to revisit that. It just goes without saying that you are pillars of our American justice system . . . the sacrifices you've made to be here. I just can't say enough to express my gratitude and my client's.

"Yes, ladies and gentlemen, Sissy Dickerson is also thankful to you. For this day is really about her . . . another victim whom we have not had a opportunity to meet as a human being. Not a defendant, not a scientific study, and not a murderess.

Not a violent, merciless, vulture like my adversary would like you to believe. No. We must take a moment to look at Sissy Dickerson, the victim. She is a woman who has been living dual roles for most of her adolescent, her teenage years, and adult life. Not only is she a woman who doesn't know who she is from one moment to the next, but she's at the mercy of these other people, their intentions . . . their willpower. We have all reviewed the psychiatric reports—an evaluation that clearly shows that Sissy Dickerson is not the killer we're after. Yes! Her body . . . her physical person may indeed have committed such vicious crimes. But the real killer is the person, or should I say, the spirit which has used Sissy's body without her knowing.

"Surely, this woman, whom reports and testimony have portrayed as someone who is mortified by the sight of blood; who literally freezes up, even while on duty, at the sight of large amounts of blood; surely this can't be the soul who chops off men's limbs or who uses ice picks to stab them to death. It can't be! I'm here to tell you that this woman doesn't know the killer. Testimony has told us that while Sissy walks and feeds a dog—a dog that she thinks is a pit bull—in fact, Sissy doesn't and never did own a pit bull. No. Sissy owns a golden retriever, folks.

"Oh, but you didn't only learn that. We've also heard on the stand, from a doctor who evaluated Sissy, that this other woman, this April Davis, has less than perfect vision. In fact, she needs glasses to read. However, Sissy's physical examination shows that she has twenty-twenty vision. The exam shows that she's in perfect health. And yet, April sneezed. She's allergic to milk and pollen in the air. Sissy has no allergies.

"Ladies and gentlemen of the jury, Sissy Dickerson has brought missing children home. In fact, she's delivered them in cases of emergencies. You heard it from her partner, Officer Maritza Garcia, how the two of them addressed domestic disputes, sometimes using expert judgement on the situation relating to the safety of children as well as the parents in these daily domestic quarrels. This woman has been a hero of the people, not a killer.

"And how can we forget that Sissy Dickerson believes she was on some national television show called *Super Woman*, and how April imagined that she was at home watching it all in the comfort of her living room. I suggest to you that this pattern of gaining and losing control of the body, the alter-identities, delusion of separateness, the physical abilities, speech variations, allergic sensitivity to foods and such other differences such as vision, taste, hearing and touch . . . Ladies and gentlemen, what about the overwhelming trauma of her childhood? Wasn't it that man who came to the stand and murdered his daughter's character, calling her a slut, a devil and unmanageable as a child?

"But then, how would this man be aware of his

daughter's so-called promiscuities if he had been away from her since she was age five? And as Dr. Janice Mifflin testified, if a common cause of multiple personality disorder is severe childhood abuse, it leaves me to wonder why Mr. Dickerson fled the household. Why is that? *Why is that?*

"On one hand this separate alter-personality says her father died when she was born. But isn't that actually Sissy Dickerson's denial of her father's existence? Why would she try to wipe any memory of her father from her mind? Could he have violated her? Could he have forced himself—"

"No! No! No Daddy! I didn't tell them. I didn't! I love you, Daddy! I'll do what you say. Please come back home!"

"I'm warning you for the last time, Miss Dickerson. One more outburst—"

"Daddy, no! Don't go!! Don't gooo!"

# RIVER

"GUARDS, PLEASE. CAN I have one moment with her before you take her?" the lawyer Quinn asked.

"Where are they takin' me, Lester?" "Somewhere in Missouri. A place where you can get better. You're still an innocent woman, Sissy."

"Better? I'm the best, Lester. Or didn't you know?" I leaned in to whisper, "Maybe you and I can have one of those attorney-client meetings in the back before I go. I could give you something nice to remember me by."

"That's quite all right, dear. I think I can manage. Ahh . . . a friend here wants to say something. Guards? Do you mind?"

"Hi, baby. Now don't you worry about a thing. They'll take good care of you, and I'll be there to visit at least once a month. Call me if you need money, books, whatever. I'll be there for you, Sissy. You have my word."

"You're Eve, aren't you?"

"Mmm-hmmm," she replied, biting her lip and spilling a tear.

I leaned into her, flashing an expression at the court officer. Do you mind?

"Eve, do me a favor and find out where that Stuart Dickerson lives. Next time we meet, I want an address, license plate number, that kind of thing . . . oh, and Eve?"

"Yes, Sissy?"

"Call me River from now on," I said, and in front of the guards, the lawyer, the government's pawns, I kissed Eve right on the mouth. I left her there, suspended in my spell as I went with the guards out of the courtroom. I couldn't help but laugh.